I0736307

Get Out Now!

Copyright © 2017 by Barbara Harrison.

ISBN: Softcover   978 – 1 – 945286 – 42 –1
        Ebooks   978 – 1 – 945286 – 31 –5
                       978 – 1 – 945286 – 32 –2
        H a r d c o v e r 978 – 1 –945286 – 33 – 9

All rights reserved. No part of this book may be reproduced or transmitted in any form or by any means, electronic or mechanical, including photocopying, recording, or by any information storage and retrieval system, without permission in writing from the copyright owner.
This is a work of fiction. Names, characters, places and incidents either are the product of the author's imagination or are used fictitiously, and any resemblance to any actual persons, living or dead, events, or locales is entirely coincidental.

Artwork by Digital Forces CC
5/15/2018

RockHill Publishing LLC
PO Box 62241
Virginia Beach, VA
23466-2241

www.rockhillpublishing.com

Get Out Now!

By Barbara Harrison

Novel – Get Out Now!
Thank You

The publishing of this novel, is due in no short measure to RockHill Publishing LLC. My grateful thanks go to Mr James Hill for taking a chance on me, and also to the Chief Editor, Athina Paris. This writing journey has had its fair share of ups and downs, but I greatly appreciate Athina taking the time to give me constructive criticism and feedback, ultimately pushing me to write a better book.

I absolutely love the detailed cover of Get Out Now!, which was personally designed by Grant, Grant and Michael of Digital Forces. Their creative ability knows no bounds and I owe them a great debt of gratitude. The essence of my story is captured in a detailed and intricate image. Thank you so very much.

From the bottom of my heart I want to thank family and friends for supporting me during my horrendous time of grief, after the loss of my beloved husband, Russel. I am still here in one piece, because they took care of me when my world was falling apart. My parents took me in when I was sick and homeless and I have never questioned their unfailing love, or that of my precious daughter and son, whom I also dearly love.

Despite the pain, there is light at the end of the tunnel. I am truly grateful for the opportunity to share my stories with the world. Writing has brought me out of a very dark place. Now I see a good future ahead.

God bless you all.

Chapter 1

Amber was shivering from head to toe. Her fingers trembled uncontrollably, as she fumbled with the locks on her overstuffed suitcase. She swiped frantically with the back of her hand at the damp fringe sticking to her brow and across her wet eyes, trying to stop a fresh flood of tears, which blurred her vision and threatened once more to stream down her pale, gaunt cheeks.

'I've got to get out now,' she thought. She slowly inhaled and smoothed back her dishevelled brown hair. It was sticky with sweat, and there was still a patch of dried blood next to her left temple. Hastily, she redid her loose, untidy ponytail with unsteady hands.

There was no longer any doubt; when he arrived home and discovered she was gone, hell would break loose! 'Bastard, you will not do this to me again,' Amber whispered angrily to herself. 'How could I ever let you abuse me? This is the last time you will ever lay a hand on me, Cade Raine.'

She stopped for a moment, leaning heavily on her suitcase, and drew in another shaky breath, trying not to aggravate her broken ribs from the vicious beating. Perspiration beaded on her swollen upper lip, the saltiness causing the open gash to sting. She inhaled sharply, the pain bringing her out of her reverie, and for a second, it cleared her whirling, terrified brain. Time was running out, and she was not ready to leave! She needed to be as far away from this house as was humanly possible—given her present physical state and capabilities—by the time he returned.

A good head-start was essential to the success of her plan, even though it was the most daunting thing she had ever done. Although she had various scenarios she could follow, this was not a last-minute decision, but her mind was foggy, barely able to think coherently. Last night's sudden and unexpected attack had caught her off-guard.

It was vital to have cash-in-hand, personal documents, her passport, and identification if she were to be successful at hiding from him and starting over elsewhere. There was a cohesive plan in place. One thing was clear and sure—to get away, as far away as she could manage and to never, ever be found by Cade again.

She quickly turned back to the task at hand, clenching her teeth, as a fresh stab of excruciating pain radiated through her body. A wave of nausea followed the unrelenting dizziness, forcing her to stand completely still, eyes closed, her trembling arms wrapped around the front of her chest, and gently cradling her damaged ribcage. She slowly drew in another breath, fighting the agony, as fear and terror threatened to engulf her already fragile mind.

As the stabbing pain, dizziness, and nausea began to subside, Amber fought the rising tide of dread and forced herself to focus on the current task. Moving hunched over, like an old woman, she returned to the suitcase to finish closing it. This time, the second lock firmly snapped shut, and as she eased the heavy bag onto the floor, it landed with a thud. Just as she pulled up the handle and it clicked into place, a loud bang came from another part of the house, sounding like a hefty door slamming closed.

Panicked and frightened, Amber held her hand to her chest and felt the wild thumping of her heart. Her breath was coming in short, quick gasps. She cocked her head to one side and held her breath for a moment. Listening intently, she waited to catch the deliberate footfall of a tall man walking down the Italian marble tiled passage. She strained her ears to catch the sound of any movement, then slowly exhaled her bated breath. Hearing nothing, she began to relax the tense muscles and calm herself. She had carefully checked every room earlier and was sure he was nowhere inside. But now, it was time to leave, before he returned and found her missing.

It was cold and miserable outside, the steadily pouring rain thrumming on the roof of the bay window. The sound reminded her that she would need her all-weather coat to cope with the wet weather predicted to last for the next several days. The gloomy pall reflected her depressed demeanour, and at that moment, she felt that all of heaven was crying with her.

Amber glanced around the room, her eyes going over things she had seen a thousand times, but today they all looked a little different. The cream and gold curtains were draped open, with the lace voile fluttering skittishly in the slightly soggy breeze. There was a matching comforter draped crookedly across a gold velour chair in front of the bay window. On the other side of the tipped-over coffee table, was a second chair brimming with a pile of cushions. In front of the cherry-wood nightstand, lay the pieces of a shattered glass lamp-base, a dark smear of blood across the cream shade. All personal items, which had once adorned the dresser, lay scattered on the floor. As Amber gazed at the jagged, shattered mirror, her distorted face startled her. The ghostly visage staring back at her was barely recognisable as her own.

Her shiny chestnut mane was a dishevelled mess and her left eye, almost swollen shut, was surrounded by red, puffy skin, and a dark blue-black contusion, which stood out starkly against her ashen face. Her top-right upper lip was also distended, and bruised, around a deep crimson gash. Smears of dry blood and more discolourations streaked her right cheek, as well as her left temple and jawline. Dark bruises on her slender, pale throat shouted out the evidence of her near strangulation. But these were only the visible marks, as the rest of the damage to her body was covered by clothing.

Once more, fury welled up inside her, not only at Cade for what he had done, but also at herself for allowing the abuse to keep on happening, time after time. She thought about all the excuses she had made for her husband. She had felt sorry for him because he was an only child, his father died when he was a young boy, he was also bipolar, and struggled with many personal demons. But, these were hardly reasons to stay in a relationship. Certainly, not in light of the evil she had personally seen revealed in the man she called her husband.

Resolutely, Amber turned away from the horrifying image and gripped the case's handle. Dragging it behind her, she left the room, gingerly negotiating her way around debris, which lay scattered about the room after last night's violent assault. She bit down on her lower lip, as it began to quiver uncontrollably and cried out in pain. Terrifying memories once more flooded her mind. She could still vividly see his iron-hard fist as the punch smashed into her delicate face. Then landing several vicious blows to her temple, eye and mouth, before slamming into her solar plexus, completely winding her, and leaving her writhing on the floor, gasping for air. But it did not stop there!

Amber began to dry retch and shake violently, recalling the never-ending brutal kicks to her stomach and ribs, as she lay confused and bleeding on the carpet. She had curled into a ball, trying to protect her face and head while white-hot pain seared through her abdomen, using all her inner strength to stop herself from crying out. The aggression would only escalate if she showed signs of weakness.

Without warning, he grabbed her by the throat, squeezing hard, dragging her upwards and shaking her around like a marionette. His grip was so fierce that it seemed clear he intended to strangle her. As defence, she clawed feverishly at his rock-solid hands throttling her. Pleadingly, she stared at the demon-like face of her husband, as she tried to free herself from his merciless grasp.

Pulling her close, he growled and hissed a single word into her ear. "Bitch."

The sickly smell of stale alcohol almost made her gag. Before she could react, he flung her violently away from him. She crashed into his bedside pedestal and fell like a ragdoll limply to the floor, passing out, and lay there in a crumpled heap.

Chapter 2

Hours passed before Amber regained consciousness. Shivering, as a result of the intense shock and clammy cold that seeped into her fragile bones, she wearily began to stir. Waves of agony wracked her body and adrenaline coursed through her veins, causing her to become aware of the night sounds, accompanied by unrelenting rain. She strained her ears to listen for noises or movements that would indicate he was still in the house, but heard nothing. After what felt like an eternity, she tried to orientate herself, to determine where she was in the room.

Her hand ran jerkily over the thick-pile carpet until it struck the base of the bed. Amber felt along until she touched the footboard and pulled herself up, struggling to her feet. Sharp pains ripped through her ribcage. She paused hesitantly, her breathing short and shallow, then perched on the edge of the bed to listen intently once more. As she strained her eyes to pierce the inky blackness, she could only just make out the glowing lights of the bedside alarm clock. It usually sat on Cade's bedside pedestal, but now lay on the floor silently blinking its time. Three o'clock in the morning.

Amber's sight gradually adjusted to the darkness and she hauled herself unsteadily upright, shuffling forward in the direction of the bathroom. She flicked on the light switch. The well-appointed bathroom, decorated in cream and gold, was brilliantly illuminated by megawatt bulbs. This room was intact, having escaped last night's ferocity unscathed.

Tentatively, she approached one of the marble basins, leaning heavily on the cold, smooth surface. She looked at herself in the mirror. The reflection horrified her, and she quickly averted her eyes, turning on the hot-water faucet. She pumped out some liquid soap, watching the fragrant foam swell up in her tremulous hand. Absentmindedly, she raised her hand up to her nose and inhaled deeply, allowing the sweet, delicate smell to permeate her entire being. For a fleeting moment, she was transported back to the previous evening, when she had last used this bathroom while preparing for bed and before her night of horror began.

Her thoughts flashed back to yesterday. Amber recalled enjoying a leisurely bubble bath, while listening to classical music and watching the dancing flames flickering on the vanilla-scented candles. She had sipped sherry from a small crystal glass. Afterwards, she put on her peach-coloured negligée with matching robe and slid her feet into soft slippers.

She had been on her way into the bedroom after her bath, ready to slip between the silky sheets, and read a few pages of a new novel before settling down to sleep, when she was alerted to the roar of a powerful engine slowing down in the street outside the house.

The sports car throttled down, glided effortlessly into the driveway, and came to a stop.

'He's home,' she thought. 'What is he doing here? He's supposed to be out of town.' She began to shake with apprehension.

Amber heard the front door slamming shut, and fearing the worst, she ran to the bed and quickly pulled the covers over herself. She picked up her book and was pretending to read when Cade walked into the room.

Amber managed to get out the words, "Hi, Honey. You're home."

There was no response.

In an attempt to cover up the fear in her voice, she continued, "I thought you were going to be out of town tonight. If I had known you were coming home I would have made supper for you. Did you get something to eat?"

Cade continued scowling ominously then without saying a word, he strode over to the bed. He grabbed her by the arms, lifting her clear of the bedding, and he began to shake her ferociously.

Amber cried out as her neck snapped wildly back and forth, and feebly attempted to pry his hands from her arms. "What are you doing?" she yelled. "Why are you doing this?"

Holding her effortlessly in his left hand, Cade smashed his fist into the left side of her face.

Her head flew sideways with the force of his blow. Still reeling in shock, she was not prepared for the next punch to her mouth, screaming as her lip split open.

Cade threw her against the dressing table.

Amber collapsed, groaning onto the ground. Then she felt Cade savagely kick her in the ribs, hammering her repeatedly, as pain seared through her body. She lay as still as she could, believing that her life depended on her silence.

Furious that his prey was not reacting or fighting back, Cade put both hands around her vulnerable neck and began to squeeze the life out of her. "Bitch," he hissed. When she became limp in his arms, he threw her into his bedside pedestal and strode angrily out of the room.

More appalling memories came flooding in. Tears welled up in her eyes, and she began to weep softly, as she recalled the brutal beating. From somewhere deep within, a primal scream was rising, which could not be contained, and the pent-up emotions from the brutal attack exploded out of her body in an agonising howl. Amber had no idea how long she screamed, but each time she ran out of air, she inhaled a ragged breath and wailed pitifully, again and again, until she was utterly exhausted.

Fearing she was going to faint from the throbbing pain, she rested her forehead on the cooling marble surface. She drew in a few shaky breaths and with each exhalation, whispered, "No. Please, no!"

Feeling the emotion slowly draining from her body, she carefully drew herself upright and leaned against the vanity slab, shuddering. Amber opened the bathroom cabinet and took out a bottle of strong painkillers. She tipped two into one hand and turned on the cold-water tap, catching water in her other hand, and drank while swallowing the pills.

She left the water running, to cool the steaming water, which was flowing into the basin. Trying to quell her tumultuous feelings, she concentrated on pumping out more soap, to softly wash her bruised and battered hands.

Cupping the soothing water, Amber rinsed her face repeatedly, gently wiping away the crusted blood from her eye, nose, and lip. After a time, she turned off the running water and reached for the towel. Carefully, she patted her hands and face dry, finding little comfort in the plush fabric, which felt rough against her battered face. She slowly inhaled a deep breath, flinching as her broken ribs made themselves felt once more.

Having cleaned herself up as best she could, Amber searched the bathroom cabinet for the tape Cade used to strap his knees when he went running. She cut a few lengths of the strapping and gingerly applied them across the left side of her ribcage, to limit movement of the fractured bones.

After one more look at her horribly beaten face, she squared her shoulders, resolutely facing the future and cautiously left the sanctuary of the bathroom.

Quietly, Amber made her way through the beautifully appointed house, adorned with expensive artworks, furniture, and fittings. Thinking to herself that this had never been a safe place for her, somewhere she could call home. It was a nightmare from a horror film.

She checked the downstairs bedrooms and bathrooms, as well as the study, lounge, and kitchen. Painstakingly, she climbed the stairs, stopping every few steps to catch her breath. When she got to the top, she stood outside the guestroom door and listened intently. No sound came from within, but still she ventured in, to be sure there was no one there. It was empty, so she made her way across the landing to the sitting room, which was also unoccupied, and walked through it to her art studio on the far side. That too was empty.

Amber looked out of the large picture window and checked the driveway. His red Ferrari was gone. He was nowhere to be found, and she began to relax a little, breathing a small sigh of relief, feeling confident that he was indeed gone. She made her way back carefully down the staircase and stopped in the kitchen to collect a cold bottle of water from the fridge. A brief glance into the garage also showed the Ferrari's usual space to be empty.

An hour had passed, and by this time, the pain shooting through Amber grew worse with each excruciating step. She returned to her bathroom and collected the bottle of painkillers.

Too afraid to sleep and not in the least bit willing to close her eyes, Amber wandered back into the main bedroom and surveyed the chaotic scene. There was no way she could get into that bed and allow herself to doze off; he might come back and too easily find her exposed and vulnerable. She decided to curl up on the floor on the far side of the room because if he looked in from the doorway, he would not be able to spot her behind the enormous, king-size bed.

Amber placed the pills and water on the floor next to a couple of big cushions. She pulled a soft blanket over herself and tried to get comfortable enough to rest. For a long time, she lay there with thoughts racing through her mind. 'Enough! I am done with this, and it is time to leave. But how do I make sure that Cade doesn't find me?'

Running through some plans in her head, she realised it was a certainty he would follow her. Although Cade had never actually said that he would kill her if she left him, she now felt sure he would. This night, Amber realised with absolute clarity that even if she stayed, he would eventually murder her anyway. It was merely a matter of time.

She was still thinking about how to make an effective escape and find a place to start a new life, without Cade locating her when the painkillers kicked in and she dozed off.

It was there, on the floor, that she found herself hours later, twisted into a foetal position on the cushions, her body screaming in agony. Locating the pills and water, she quickly downed two more, before putting her plans into action.

Finally, Amber had made the decision to pack her things and leave, and unless, by some fluke, he returned home and tried to stop her, getting out was precisely what she was going to do.

Chapter 3

The wheels of the trolley-case clacked loudly on the tiles, echoing eerily, as Amber pulled it behind her. Rucksack on her back, she made her way down the passage towards the inter-leading door to the garage. Passing the brass key holder on the wall, she automatically reached out to take the keys to her Mercedes. Then, she hesitated, her hand hovering indecisively over the topaz keyring. Instead, she grabbed a different set, one with a copper keyring, the one for the BMW X5, instinctively realising this was a practical choice, as it could drive over a variety of terrains. It would also provide reasonably comfortable sleeping space, and still have room for other necessary items, such as camping equipment, food, and water.

She moved as quickly as her injuries would allow, and made her way through the kitchen, stopping briefly to fill a couple of bags with non-perishable items and bottles of water, then continued to the wooden door that led to the double garage adjoining the house. Amber unlocked the door, dragged her heavy bag through, locked the door behind her, and absentmindedly pocketed the key.

Unlocking the trunk, Amber used her strong arms and legs to heave the weighty suitcase into the back of the SUV, doing her best to avoid jarring her broken ribs. But that was impossible, and excruciating pain stabbed through her body as she lifted the bag into the air. She dropped it into the car and let out an agonised groan, panting with the exertion and unrelenting agony knifing through her ribcage. She gripped the side of the car and stood for a moment with her eyes closed, gritting her teeth, and taking short, shallow gasps, waiting for the throbbing to recede. Then, she carefully placed the bags of groceries alongside the luggage.

Purposefully, Amber slammed the trunk shut and headed steadily for the driver's door, leaning on the car for support as she went. She eased herself in carefully and started the car, pressed the remote to open the garage door, and cautiously reversed the powerful vehicle out into the driveway. Lowering the garage door, she backed into the street and drove away from the house without once looking back.

Her mind raced, mentally plotting the route, trying to elect the best way to avoid bumping into him. Decision made, she travelled in the opposite direction to his art gallery in Cape Town, winding through suburban streets and unfamiliar roads, until she was over the mountain and headed away from Hout Bay.

Although she had taken the precaution of wrapping a scarf around her head and covering her eyes with sunglasses, Amber knew he would instantly recognise the car if he saw it. There was also the chance he would employ the police force's assistance to track it down, once he realised she had left in the X5. She was torn between using the vehicle as a temporary home on the run, or ditching it and utilising other forms of transport. However, she still had a few hours to decide, because hopefully, if he had gone to work as usual, he would not return home before nightfall, and she would be long gone by then.

After a couple of hours, she was finally out on the quiet beach road and she put her foot down on the accelerator, trying to build up as many miles as possible between herself and her assailant, as quickly as she could. Amber knew she had to be vigilant to ensure she was consistently ahead of the game if she were to make a clean get-away and find a safe place to stay.

The road was bordered on the left by dunes and scrub vegetation, and on the right, was the sandy beach and ocean, but still no respite from the unremitting downpour. Everything was grey and sodden, reflecting her sombre mood. Her thoughts were solemn, reflecting on the life she was leaving behind.

Her ten-year marriage to Cade Raine had been tumultuous and sometimes horrific. For a sobering moment, Amber wondered how she had managed to survive. More than that, she could not believe she had waited this long to leave.

Reasoning with herself, it was clear that it had not all been bad during that time. There had been times of relative peace and odd moments of real happiness. In the end, it was the dreadful times, which had become more frequent, that had finally outweighed the good days.

Despite being married to a very wealthy man, Amber had lived an isolated and tiny, little life. She began to feel rage strengthening her resolve, as she thought about all that had been taken from her.

Far out in the ocean, a humpback whale breached, puffing a plume of water out of its blow-hole and then crashing back into the water. This was whale season in the Western Cape, and the colossal ocean mammals were on their annual pilgrimage north. Amber barely noticed, her mind entirely focused on her attempt to successfully escape the reach of her brutal attacker.

Her current dilemma was whether or not to take the scenic route along the coastline, via Hermanus, or to cut across inland, towards Knysna. She decided not to continue on the quieter roads, but instead to take as direct a route as possible from there. It would probably be best to head towards Somerset West, get onto the N2 highway, and go as far as she could before nightfall.

Her mind still felt somewhat foggy and she surmised it could be due to concussion from the beating. She was also feeling dizzy and nauseous and desperately needed some coffee with plenty of sugar and a hot meal. It would also be a good idea to top up with petrol, as the tank was running low. As she drove through Heidelberg, she saw a filling station on the left, and quickly pulled in. There was a sign for a restaurant a little way up the road.

'Great,' she thought, 'I can make a quick stop and be back on the road in no time.'

It was still raining, although it had lessened slightly. Tugging the jacket hood over her head, Amber grabbed her backpack and eased herself out of the car, hugging the side of the building as she made her way to the entrance.

The country-style eatery was warm and cosy, with only a few patrons near the front. That was a relief, but still, she decided to take a seat on the opposite side of the room. She quickly perused the menu then made her way to a booth, where she placed her order. Spotting a sign for the Ladies' Room, she went to freshen up and wash her hands before returning to the welcoming warmth of the restaurant.

Coffee was waiting upon her return, and after adding three sachets of brown sugar, Amber took a long sip of the warm brew, the comforting liquid soothing her parched and aching throat. She sat silently, her eyes closed for a few minutes, trying to relax, then realised the waiter had placed the sandwich in front of her and disappeared back into the kitchen.

As she began to eat slowly, Amber discovered that she was famished and thinking back on the last twenty-four hours, she realised that the last proper meal she had consumed was lunch the day before. She had not felt hungry in the evening and merely snacked on crackers and cheese with her sherry in the bath. The thought of food had not crossed her mind this morning; her throat was so sore and swollen it made even drinking water difficult. The only thing she had been able to think about was getting out of that house, and far away, as quickly as possible.

The warm food and coffee quickly thawed her insides and Amber began to feel better, less light-headed, and dizzy. Her broken ribs ached persistently, but if she moved carefully, she could almost avoid the pain that would rip through her if she manoeuvred too hastily. Now that she had eaten something, she could take more painkillers, and hopefully, they would provide some respite from the nagging discomfort.

The bill had been left on the table with the food, and she counted out the cash she owed, adding a good tip, and tucked the money into the faux leather folder. It was time to put some decent miles between her and her tormentor.

Moving as fast as she could, Amber climbed back into the vehicle and continued her journey along the highway, mentally planning her course. She did not know where she was going to stay, only that she had to be far, far away by nightfall, and hopefully somewhere he would never think to look.

Chapter 4

Hours passed rapidly with the powerful SUV eating up the miles. It was evening, and it would not be long before the sun would set, but none of that was going to make a difference since the sky was still cloud-covered and although the downpour had diminished, it had not stopped. It was getting dark, and Amber did not want to keep driving through the night, especially in the rain. She was shivering due to the cold and damp, so she turned up the heat. Rest was now essential to give her time to heal and recover, as well as to allow her to recharge energy levels to keep going.

She did not know the area she was driving through at all. What Amber did know was that she needed to find a place to spend the night. As she drove, her eyes darted left and right, peering through the grey drizzle for the promising sign of a hotel or guesthouse. Her ribs ached relentlessly, and she needed pain relief. She was also hungry again and utterly fatigued. She had headed towards Port Elizabeth but decided to push on farther to increase the distance between herself and Hout Bay.

Two more hours passed and headed out the other side of Grahamstown, she contemplated eating some of the provisions she had brought along, to lay out the sleeping bag, and catch some shut-eye. By a stroke of good luck, as she was looking for a safe place to pull over and park the BMW for the night, she saw instead a small crooked sign offering bed and breakfast at cheap prices.

'Perfect,' she thought and experienced a small stab of conscience, when she realised that not too long ago, she would never have considered staying at any place less than a five-star hotel when she travelled. In some ways, she had been spoiled by her life with Cade, but money and luxury could never make up for the abuse she had suffered at his hands.

The entrance to the small house was around the back and off the side-street, which was good news. The vehicle would not be visible from the main road, providing they had a place for her to park.

As she pulled into the driveway, Amber saw one spot alongside the single garage, covered with a pergola, which was overrun with creepers. 'Even better,' she thought and drove the SUV under the cover. Yanking her hood up again, Amber pulled on her gloves and grabbed her rucksack. Moving as swiftly as she could toward the only visible entry, she rapped loudly on the peeling wooden door.

Fortunately, there was a small awning over the doorstep, and she was mostly out of the rain, but it was still cold, despite her coat and gloves. She stamped her feet on the concrete step and rubbed her hands together, praying that someone would open the door soon. But no one came.

Desperately, she knocked harder and longer on the door, calling "Hello. Is anybody there?" as loudly as she could.

It seemed like an eternity before she heard the creak of a wooden floorboard behind the door and guessed that the owner of the cottage was peering at her through the spy-hole. She threw off the hood of her jacket and lifted her face upwards. Amber smiled awkwardly and tried to look non-threatening. After standing like that for a couple of minutes, the door creaked and gradually opened inwards.

A small elderly woman, with silvery-white hair and dressed in a floral dressing gown greeted her with the words, "Yes, may I help you?"

"Please," Amber replied, "I am travelling a long way, and I need a place to stay for the night. I saw your sign and stopped to enquire about lodging. Sorry it is so late, but I have not seen any other accommodation on my route."

"Well," quavered the old lady, "it is very late. To be honest, I don't do the room and board anymore… not since my husband died. I just never got around to taking down the sign."

"Ma'am, my name is Amber, and I hate to trouble you, but I am utterly exhausted! I am desperate to get some sleep; I will pay you generously for the inconvenience," she implored, while slowly sliding the sunglasses off her face and allowing the woman to catch a glimpse of her black eye.

"Oh, my!" said the silver-haired woman, drawing in a sharp breath, and taking an involuntary step backwards. "Whatever happened to you? Were you in an accident?"

"I guess you could say that," Amber responded. "It's a very long story. Please, may I come inside? And if you have time to listen, I will tell you all about it."

The woman hesitated for another moment then opened the door wide and motioned for Amber to enter. "Yes, do come in," she said. "My name is Gloria McBride. The place may look shabby, but I assure you it's clean. Follow the short passage to the end, and that will be your room for the night. I'll bring bedding and towels in a minute. There is a bathroom alongside the room, which we will have to share. So, feel free to freshen up while I put on the kettle. Can I interest you in a cup of hot cocoa?"

"Yes, please, Gloria, I would love some. Thank you for letting me in, I am so grateful and appreciate whatever accommodation you offer. I'll drop my things in the bedroom and join you in the kitchen," replied Amber.

"Right you are," said Gloria and shuffled into the area alongside the front door.

Relieved, Amber removed her all-weather jacket, hung it on a peg opposite the kitchen door, and hauled her backpack into the small room at the end of the passage. It was sparsely furnished, but the bed looked comfortable enough, and Gloria was right, the place was immaculately clean.

Dumping her bag on the only chair in the corner, she went in search of the bathroom and almost bumped into Gloria, who was approaching from the opposite direction with pillows, sheets, a crocheted blanket, down duvet, and two towels clutched in her arms.

"Here," Gloria offered, "these are for you. If there is anything else you need, just ask."

"Thank you so much," Amber said, relieving Gloria of the bedding, and returned to the room to prepare it for the night. She removed the patchwork coverlet from the bed, folded it, and draped it over the back of the chair. Then quickly, while being careful to protect her ribcage, she made the bed and headed back to the bathroom with her hand towel and bag of toiletries.

The tiny bathroom was yellowing white and old-fashioned, with a tatty lace curtain adorning the window. It had probably been quite pretty back in the day, but time had taken its toll. The old pedestal basin was spotless, and apart from a small crack, appeared to still be in decent condition. Amber opened the hot faucet and washed her hands while waiting for the water to heat up, then splashed her face a few times and dried off with the mustard hand towel, which was scented with lavender.

She carefully examined her split lip and badly bruised eye in the tarnished mirror. The light was warm and diffused, which softened the look of her haggard face. Thankfully, the swelling on her lip had gone down significantly, and the gash was no longer bleeding. The black eye looked dreadful, but puffiness had also reduced, and the eye was a little more open. Amber patted some concealer onto the blue-black areas and smoothed it gently into the skin, minimising the harshness of the welts. Then, she slicked a little bit of beeswax onto her lips and ran her fingers through the tangled hair. Smoothing it down as best she could, she once more tied it up into a ponytail. After inhaling another calming breath and a final check of her reflection, she went to find Gloria in the kitchen.

Gloria was placing a steaming hot mug of cocoa on a crocheted coaster on the whitewashed table as her unexpected guest entered the room. She pointed to a wooden chair, which matched the one in the bedroom, motioning for Amber to take a seat.

"Feeling better?" asked Gloria.

"Much better, thank you. This cocoa smells delicious."

"Would you like to eat a slice of homemade toasted bread with honey?"

"That sounds wonderful; I am starving!"

A few minutes later, both were quietly munching on the warm toast and sipping the soothing hot drink. They sat in amicable silence for a while, even if complete strangers, each lost in their thoughts until they finished the food and beverage.

Amber downed some more painkillers.

"I know you have quite a story to tell, but I can also see how exhausted you are and I feel this is not the time to talk about it. If you are willing, feel free to tell me in the morning over breakfast."

Amber's eyes welled with fresh tears. "Gloria, you are an angel! I am too tired to think straight right now, but I will gladly tell you in the morning, as long as you are okay with a very early start?"

"Not a problem. I am always up at about five anyway. I'll have breakfast ready for around six, if that's fine with you?"

"Perfect! Thank you, Gloria, I cannot tell you how grateful I am that you took me in."

"I'm glad I could help. Now get yourself to bed and try to get some rest. I'll quickly rinse these dishes and then see you in the morning."

"Goodnight, Gloria, sleep well."

Gloria shooed Amber out of the room, "You too, Honey! And sweet dreams."

Amber yawned as she made her way back to the little room at the front of the house facing the main road. Through the open curtains, she saw it was still raining, and the single yellow streetlamp looked hazy past the misted glass.

A feeling of panic rose in her throat as she stared outside and was reminded of why she was in this place. Then taking a deep breath, she forced the fear back down and carefully closed the faded fabric drapes. Turning back to the bed, she stripped down to her underwear, slid into the surprisingly comfortable bed, and snuggled under the thick down duvet.

'To sleep, perchance to dream—' she thought, as a tiny shiver ran down her spine. 'Wonder where I heard that line?' Before she could consciously recall that the line was from Hamlet's 'To be, or not to be?' speech, she was sound asleep, snoring gently and rhythmically, as Gloria noted when she popped her head into the room on her way to bed.

Chapter 5

Terrified screams ripped through the silence.

"Noooo! No, please don't. I'm begging you, don't do this! Noooo!" Amber tossed her head from side to side, clutching at the bedclothes with scarred hands, knuckles white with tension and legs flailing beneath the covers. She was crying and whimpering like a frightened puppy, tears streaming down her pale face.

"Shhh, shhh," soothed Gloria, her gentle hand smoothing the damp hair off the sweat-beaded forehead.

Amber's eyes flew open. "Who is there?"

"Gloria, Honey. You were having a terrible nightmare. I heard you screaming and came in to check," she responded. "Are you alright now?"

"I… I think so," stammered Amber. "Where am I?"

"My name is Gloria McBride, and you are staying with me in my cottage. You stopped here last night looking for a place to sleep. Do you recall doing that?"

The glazed look began to lift from Amber's startled eyes, and her erratic breathing returned to normal. Her clenched hands released the down-filled comforter, and her legs stilled their involuntary movements. "Yes, I do. I'm sorry I disturbed you. I'm okay now. You can go back to bed."

"Don't fuss over me, I'm fine and already wide-awake. It's four in the morning, and it won't do me any harm to be up a bit earlier today," chided Gloria. "Besides, I have some things to take care of. You can go back to sleep if you want to."

"No, I think I'm going to get up and have a shower. Is that alright with you?"

Gloria smiled kindly. "Take your time, Honey. Meantime, I'll put the kettle on, and we can have some coffee when you're ready."

"Bless you, Gloria," whispered Amber. "I won't be too long."

Amber eased herself slowly out of bed as Gloria shuffled out of the room and towards the kitchen. Her entire body was stiff and sore, the broken ribs jagging sharply as she drew herself upright. She held her chest tightly with the left arm, as she moved cautiously out of the bedroom, and towards the bathroom.

She felt a little agitated. Her mind wandering to the terrible cruelty her abusive husband had inflicted on her, not just last night, but also during their ten years of marriage. Her thoughts swung back and forth. First, she was angry with Cade; that he had used her as a punching bag. Then she was mad at herself, for allowing it to happen

Chiding herself as she undressed in the bathroom, she thought, 'I did not deserve this. No matter what I said or did, it did not warrant being beaten and strangled to within an inch of my life.'

Tears began to well up in her eyes but drawing upon a hidden reservoir of strength, she turned on the shower. Stiffening her shoulders, she blinked away the moist droplets clinging to her eyelashes, while waiting for the water to heat up, and carefully removed the sticky strapping tape from her ribcage.

Within a few minutes, she stood inside the old, yellowing bathtub, enveloped in a cloud of steam and a soothing shower sprayed warm water over her aching body. As she lathered up with the old-fashioned Magnolia soap, she found that some of the pain and tension began to ebb away. Incongruous as it seemed, there was one thing that made Amber giggle, and it was the pale-green, plastic curtain that clung to her wet body every time she moved.

Then she started humming softly to herself, while she methodically washed from head to toe, scrubbing intently; as if trying to erode the memory of everything that had gone before. The water began to run cold, and she realised with a start, that she was still standing in the shower and had used all the hot water. Feeling guilty, she turned off the taps and wrapped herself in the threadbare bath towel Gloria had given her the night before.

She dried quickly and after carefully applying fresh tape to her fractured ribs, she dressed once more in the clothes she had worn yesterday. They were not too clean, but that was the least of her concerns, with so many more important things to think about.

Her ablutions completed and hair pulled back into its familiar ponytail, Amber returned to the bedroom. She straightened up the bed and checked for any stray belongings. Her headscarf lay on the floor, where it had fallen off her bag. She bent down gingerly to pick it up and draped it loosely around her neck as she made her way to the warm, cosy kitchen.

"Good shower?" enquired Gloria, as she placed a mug of hot coffee in front of Amber.

Spooning two teaspoons of brown sugar into the liquid and stirring well, Amber said sheepishly, "Wonderful, but I am very sorry, I used all your hot water."

"Don't you worry yourself about it, it's a small water tank. It will fill up quickly and be hot enough by the time I want to use it later. I am pleased you enjoyed a nice clean-up. I still have homemade bread if you'd like a repeat of the toast and honey; plus a few berries, and Greek yoghurt for breakfast?"

"That sounds soooo good!" said Amber, while breathing in the reassuring smell of the aromatic coffee and taking a satisfying swallow.

Placing the food on the table, Gloria sat down. Then spooning some fresh fruit over her bowl of yoghurt, she looked at her houseguest, and in a soft voice, said, "Okay, Honey, tell me your story. What was that dreadful nightmare about and why are you on the run?"

Chapter 6

Amber thought reflectively for a moment and took another long sip of her coffee before she gazed sadly at Gloria and began to speak, in a low, tremulous tone.

"I guess I should start at the beginning, ten years ago, when I met my husband," she offered. "I was in my final year of study, for a Fine Arts degree, at the University of Cape Town. One day, a group of us decided to take a drive over the mountain to Hout Bay. We intended to have a fish lunch at one of the local restaurants, before taking a look at an exhibition of local artwork on the beach." A few moments of silence followed as she paused to gather her thoughts.

"Go on," prompted Gloria.

"It was a beautiful spring day in the Cape. The air was crisp, with a sea breeze, and soft puffy clouds floated high in the powder blue sky. We decided to make our way through the remarkable, old suburb of Constantia, with its towering oak trees and Cape Dutch architecture, before entering the scenic Chapman's Peak Road, a few kilometres from our destination.

"As we drove down the winding mountain, the picturesque Hout Bay came into view. The ocean was a deep, cerulean blue, with frothy, white waves rolling up onto a golden, sandy shore. We parked close to the restaurant on the beachfront and walked laughing and joking along the pathway leading to the tables overlooking the bay.

"We ordered our food and drink and settled down to have a fun time together. The talk was light and jovial, with much bantering going back and forth between the members of the group.

"After enjoying a tasty lunch, we all wandered down to the beach to view the art on display, by a local artist, Cade Raine, who was well-known for his bold and beautiful oil paintings of the stunning Western Cape scenery. Somehow, he always managed to make his work unique and different, not kitsch, or ordinary in any way. His renditions of the Cape seas were frequently wild and stormy, and Table Mountain looked dark and mysterious with its cloud tablecloth rolling off the mountain in multiple shades of grey.

"I remember standing in front of one of his incredible Hout Bay paintings and being captivated by the way he had depicted the dappled play of sunlight on the ocean, which was varying shades of azure and indigo. The water was wild, and it appeared as if the small defenceless fishing boats were being tossed about on the waves. I jumped, as I heard a deep male voice next to my ear…

"Do you like it?" asked the stranger.

Startled, I turned to face the tall, well-tanned man, who had a thick thatch of corn-coloured hair, the top bleached lighter by the sun. His eyes were ice-blue, and his firm muscular arms folded across his broad chest. He was wearing a white, button-up, cotton shirt, which was open at the top to reveal a deeply bronzed neck and some curling, dark-blond hair. The man wore a pair of beige-coloured Chinos, which seemed to cling to his tautly-muscled legs. His brown feet were bare and covered in beach sand.

I let out an involuntary gasp at the statuesque beauty of this man towering above me and turned quickly back to the painting, trying to regain my composure.

"Yes, yes," I stammered, "I love it. The way light dances on the water and the waves crash onto the shore… It looks exciting and dangerous!"

"I am pleased that you are impressed with my work," drawled the handsome man's voice.

"Your work? You are the artist… Cade Raine?" I asked breathlessly. "I am so thrilled to meet you! I am an ardent admirer of your art and had previously only seen a couple of canvasses… I was so impressed that I wanted to attend this exhibition. Now, here I am, meeting you in person," I babbled nervously. I extended my arm, offering a polite handshake.

"I am most flattered," Cade replied, and reaching out, took Amber's right hand and brought it to his mouth, pressing his sensuous lips softly against the back. "May I ask your name?"

She shivered and pulled her hand away, as if it had been burned, rubbing it self-consciously with her fingers. Blushing scarlet and stuttering nervously, she said, "Am… Amber. Amber Light."

"What a beautiful name," drawled Cade, a slight smile curving his full lips. "It suits you perfectly, with your chestnut hair and honey-gold eyes." With a long slim forefinger, he gently stroked the side of Amber's jaw, then tilted her head upward with the tip of his finger under her chin. "I don't often do portraits, but I would love to paint yours. Would you sit for me, Amber Light?" he asked playfully.

Blushing furiously and struck totally speechless, all I could do was nod and smile.

Removing his hand from her face, Cade reached into his back pocket and drew out a business card. "Take this, and call me. We can make a date to start your portrait."

I took the card, my hand shaking slightly, "Thank you, Mr Raine, I will. I'll call."

"You can call me Cade." He smiled enigmatically and turned to walk away. "Enjoy the rest of the exhibition. See you soon," he threw over his shoulder as he wandered over to speak to other people admiring the displayed works.

Feeling flustered and somewhat foolish, I tucked the gold embossed business card into the pocket of my jeans and brushed a few stray strands of long hair behind one ear. I took a few deep breaths to calm my erratically beating heart, and as I walked over to join my friends, I felt weak at the knees.

Naturally, my friends were curious and bombarded me with questions. "Who were you talking to? Who was that gorgeous hunk? What did he say? Why were you blushing, and looking so embarrassed?"

I answered, spilling out replies like a glass of champagne bubbling over. "That, was the artist who painted this collection, Cade Raine. He wants me to sit for him… Cade Raine wants to paint my portrait. He said I could call him Cade. He's so gorgeous to look at I could hardly speak."

"All my friends thought the idea was fantastic and encouraged me to call him the following week, which I did, and we set a date to meet at the same beach to discuss the portrait."

"Let me pour us a fresh cup of coffee, and then you can continue," said Gloria.

Chapter 7

In reflective silence, Amber finished her breakfast, while Gloria brewed a fresh pot of coffee. Neither spoke until the two steaming mugs were on the kitchen table again.

"Go on, tell me what happened after that first exciting meeting with the renowned artist, Cade Raine," coaxed Gloria.

"I met Cade at the beach late in the afternoon on the appointed day and discovered that he had brought a blanket, picnic basket, and backpack with him," continued Amber. "We walked a little way along the shore to a fairly secluded spot and laid out the rug and picnic fare on the warm, soft sand."

To my delight, he produced two crystal champagne glasses and a chilled bottle of sparkling peach wine. Cade then laid out a smorgasbord of cheese and crackers, together with a bowl of fresh cherries and thin mint chocolates. A little frisson of excitement ran down my spine. Of course, I was stunned; this good-looking man… a talented artist had gone to quite some trouble for me!

He filled the champagne glasses and handed me one. Then we placed a few crackers with cheese and some cherries on small cream and gold porcelain plates. In-between sips of the peach bubbly and snacks, we began to talk, sharing information, and learning about each other.

I discovered that Cade was thirty years old, an only child of incredibly wealthy parents, with his widowed mother being taken care of in a very costly Home for Alzheimer patients. His mother had also been an artist but had struggled terribly with depression all her life, and her artworks were dark, sombre, and scary. With the result that she had not sold many and her work was not well known, even though she had painted prolifically. Most of her macabre paintings were apparently stored in an outside room next to his house because Cade had not had the heart to get rid of them. His father had died, after a fatal fall down a flight of stairs, when Cade was about seven years old. He did not remember much about him, except that he was a very cold, hard man, and a workaholic. Brick had little time for a quiet, tow-head boy and limited tolerance for a sad, wretched wife.

When it was my turn, I told him about my wonderful parents who had meant everything to me, until they were killed in a car crash when I was only ten years old. I described my sweet older sister, Crystal, who was married, with two children, and lived in White River in the Northern Province. Crystal took care of me and my brother, Lane, the middle child, after our parents died. Lane was working and travelling in England. Because both lived far away, I did not see much of my siblings. Our parents had left us with a fairly comfortable inheritance, so I was able to keep myself and pay for my Arts Degree at Cape Town University.

While I was talking, Cade reached into his backpack and brought out a box of charcoal pencils and a sketchpad. He started drawing me in rough outlines on one of the finely textured white sheets. A perfect rendering of my face appearing on the page beneath his strong, masculine hand.

We talked for hours and shared many things about ourselves, and later, sitting in comfortable silence, Cade and I watched as the sun slipped behind the mountain circling Hout Bay, in a glorious display of gold, orange, and pink.

Then dropping the sketchpad onto the blanket and standing up in one fluid movement, Cade held out a perfectly-manicured artist's hand, and gently lifted me to my feet. He tugged me towards him and moulded my pliable body against his well-built, muscular chest.

I felt giddy and excited, closing my eyes against the intensity of his blue gaze. I knew it was coming, but it still surprised me when I felt his full, soft lips press firmly onto mine. It was a slow, teasing kiss that lasted only seconds, and left me breathless and longing for more. My knees were weak, and I leaned against him, drawing strength from his arms holding me up. Gently, he moved away from me. Without speaking, we packed the picnic basket, blanket and sketch pad, and walked hand in hand back up the beach to the parking lot.

Cade popped the trunk on the red Ferrari and dumped everything in, then turning to me, he said, "Follow me in your car, I want you to come home with me."

My mind said, 'No, don't do it, it's too soon!' But my heart was fluttering like a butterfly caught in a breeze and was definitely not listening. Simply smiling and nodding, I climbed into my Honda Civic and followed him through the winding roads into a suburb of Hout Bay.

At the end of a quiet cul-de-sac, was a curved driveway alongside an enormous house, which was difficult to see against the side of the mountain in the dimness of twilight.

Cade pulled into the garage, and I stopped outside behind him. I followed him to the massive wooden front door, into which was carved the silhouette of a roaring lion. Little did I know that, in time, the engraving would speak volumes. The interior had cream, marble floor tiles leading the eye to a curving staircase on one side of the entrance hall, with a gorgeous black-leaf balustrade and railing, and up to a dome-like ceiling with an old-fashioned, crystal chandelier suspended in the middle. In stark contrast, the walls were mostly bare and painted dull grey.

As I wandered down the hallway, I glanced into the first room on my left; it was a kitchen, clean but devoid of any kitchen utensils or décor. Puzzled, I continued to follow

33

him. He had passed the staircase and walked into an area at the end of the passageway. There was a large room on the right, which I took to be the lounge, and was also sparsely furnished with mismatched furniture.

Further mystified, I shook my head and walked into what turned out to be the main bedroom of the house. A once plush grey carpet was looking a bit tatty, and while the king-size bed had a pretty silver and grey bedcover, it was devoid of accent cushions or even a throw blanket. The curtains, which Cade was closing, were dark charcoal with a vertical silver stripe. He then switched on a silver and grey lamp on the intricately carved bedside pedestal.

Before I could ponder further over the minimal furniture and dated décor and fittings, Cade strode across the room and sweeping me up in his arms, lay me lightly on the large bed. Cradling my head in his hand, he then proceeded to kiss me until my head swam with giddiness, and my heart thumped right out of my chest.

Amber stopped telling her tale and sat quietly for a moment, tears welling up in her eyes and spilling down her cheeks. A once beautiful memory, now tarnished by years of angst and torment.

Gloria held out a box of tissues for Amber to help herself and stroked the pretty hair for a moment, then said, "Go on, get it out, Honey, tell me what happened."

"I suppose I don't need to tell you what took place next. I'm sure you can guess," replied Amber. "We made love all night long. He knew just where to kiss and touch me, all over my body, while he whispered sweet words in my ear.

Cade was the first man I had ever been with, and our union seemed flawless. He loved me so tenderly, and we only fell asleep in each other's arms in the small hours of the morning. When we awoke, I knew without a doubt that I was utterly and deliriously in love with this incredible man. He had been gentle, yet sure, and strong without hurting me."

"And Cade, how did he feel?"

"I believed he felt the same and he certainly acted like someone in love. He was everything and more than I ever dreamed of in a man. He treated me like fine china, was kind, compassionate, thoughtful, funny, interesting… I could go on and on. He seemed perfect, and that probably should have been the first warning sign. As they say, if something seems too good to be true, it usually is."

"So, what caused you to change your mind?"

"Nothing of any real significance initially, although there were things that I didn't consciously notice in the beginning. A few small eccentricities did not register straightaway but began to add up to something seriously strange over time. Looking back, red flags were waving furiously! If only I had noticed and thought things through more carefully."

"What kind of things, Amber?"

"He began to isolate me from my friends and family; he did not want me spending time with anyone but him; the haste in which we were married; his sudden mood swings and the fact that he did not want me to meet his mother, amongst other anomalies. The separation from the outside world was slow and insidious and took a long time for me to comprehend the implications."

"I understand. And from the little I know about it, one of the first things abusers do is isolate the object of their obsession from loved ones. What happened after that first night?"

"I moved in with Cade immediately, and one incredible, unreal day, followed the other. We were so madly in love, that three weeks later we were married."

Chapter 8

The first glorious night, turned into glorious days. Just like that, I dropped out of University and made my home with Cade. He seemed besotted with me, and I was smitten with him. We could not get enough of each other. If we were not making love, we took long walks on the beach or up the mountain behind the house, holding hands and talking.

At home, I sat for Cade, as he worked on the portrait and even that silence, the artist engrossed in his work, was fulfilling. We discussed art, and I felt that I discovered more about painting in those few weeks than I had learned in years at University.

We cooked together in his well-equipped kitchen. Although it had seemed sparse and empty that first night, I discovered he had all the latest appliances, tucked away in the beautiful Maple-wood cupboards. We ate off the elegant cream and gold porcelain dinner service, which had previously belonged to his mother, as had most of the antique furniture.

Cade and I piled our plates with the delicious food we made, and accompanied it with one of the expensive wines from his well-stocked wine cellar, in beautiful crystal glasses. Then we ran upstairs to the comfortable sitting room, which had huge glass sliding doors leading out onto a covered patio, where we ate our meal and enjoyed the stunning view.

One evening, barely a week after I had moved in, we went for a romantic, moonlit walk on the beach. Standing at the water's edge, we gazed transfixed at the giant luminous moon sparkling on the deep blue ocean, creating a magical silver pathway from shore to horizon. I stood in front of Cade, leaning back against his broad muscular chest with his strong arms wrapped around me, pulling me close.

Then slowly but deliberately, he turned me around to face him, gently cradling my face in his smooth, firm hand and began to kiss me with such passion and intensity I went weak and felt myself swoon. He lifted his head, looking directly into my eyes and said in his deep, sexy voice, "Amber, I love you. Will you marry me?"

If he had not been holding me up, I think I would have collapsed at his feet, from shock. Although my brain told me no relationship should move that fast, I couldn't stop myself answering him breathlessly, "Oh, yes, Cade. Yes, I will."

Holding me effortlessly with one hand, he reached into his pocket with the other. He solemnly presented me with a long red suede box.

I opened it to reveal a gold necklace complete with a teardrop pearl and diamond pendant.

"Please accept this as a betrothal gift for the time being. I will give you a proper engagement ring in the very near future. This necklace belonged to my mother, who gave it to me some years back. Now, I want you to have it."

Tears welled up and threatened to overflow, as Cade fixed the exquisite piece of jewellery around my neck. I whispered, "Thank you," and threw my arms around his neck.

Then he kissed me again until my head spun once more with desire and my heart beat so wildly I thought it would fly right out of my chest.

As we walked back to his car for the drive home, we held hands and made wedding plans. Cade wanted to elope and be married as quickly as possible.

"What about our friends and family?" I asked. "Surely, there are people you'd like to celebrate the day with us"

"Yes, there are," he replied, "but it will take too long to arrange a large elaborate affair, and I want to make you my wife as soon as I can. I'd like to have a private ceremony, with just the two of us, and perhaps on our return from our honeymoon, we can have a big party with all the people we would have invited to the wedding?"

"Okay…" I said hesitantly. "What do you have in mind?"

Looking intently into my eyes, he asked, "How do you feel about an island wedding, right on the beach?"

I drew in a quick breath in surprise and answered excitedly. "Really? Are you serious? Which island did you have in mind?"

"I was thinking, Hawaii?"

"Oh…" I gushed. "That is wonderful! I would love that!"

"Then let's go home and chat about it over a nightcap."

My brain was whirling with thoughts and ideas, and I felt giddy with excitement. I was, however, in two minds about this proposal. I had always wanted the traditional church wedding, in a long white dress and veil, with my friends and family in attendance to celebrate our union. Nonetheless, I also knew I wanted to be with this man forever and become his wife as soon as possible. So I put aside my concerns and concentrated instead on the happiness I felt at the thought of spending my future with him.

This handsome, intelligent, talented man was like an addictive drug, and I could not get enough of him. I was evidently under his mesmerising spell and his every word was my command. To use a somewhat well-worn cliché, I felt that he completed me. I needed him as much as the air I breathed.

In less than a week, after a flurry of arrangements, our wedding was planned at a gorgeous hotel in Hawaii. Because of the time constraints, I decided to go with the typical island theme, including tropical flowers and colours, and the hotel agreed to prepare an intimate wedding dinner for the two of us on the beach, after the outdoor ceremony.

I went shopping for a wedding dress and selected one in silky, pale cream, with a full skirt, gathered at the waist, and falling in soft folds to my feet. The top was fitted with a sweetheart neckline and gathered off-the-shoulder sleeves. A long, silk sash went around the waist and tied in a loose knot, the ends hanging down at the back of the skirt. I chose a soft, flowing veil, which would attach to a circle of fresh flowers for hair adornment. A pair of flat gold ballet pumps completed the elegant ensemble.

The idea of getting married without my loved ones present made me a little sad, but I was so excited about our island wedding that I put those thoughts to the back of my mind and focussed on spending the rest of my life with the man of my dreams.

Chapter 9

The golden sun was just peeping over the horizon when I woke up on the day we were leaving for America. Later on, we would travel to Hawaii. Cade was still sleeping, so I quietly put on my dressing gown and made my way to the kitchen. Popping the kettle on, I made a cup of steaming coffee and grabbed a muesli rusk from the container, then went upstairs to sit on the patio.

The sea air was fresh, and the scene before me bathed in the glorious golden glow of morning light, the ocean glittering and sparkling beneath the sun's rays. The scenic view made my heart dance. It dawned on me that we could quite easily have had our marriage ceremony right there on Hout Bay beach. A wedding in Hawaii was very extravagant. Shaking off the unwelcome thoughts, I turned my concentration back to actual plans for the day.

My mind ran through a mental checklist of everything that still needed to be done before we left for the airport. I had completed most of my packing the previous day, after I had collected my wedding dress from the seamstress, Mandy.

The lustrous, cream gown I had chosen was elegant and beautiful, if a little plain, so I decided to seek out someone who could add some glitz and glamour. Mandy was a real gem; she attached tiny cream-coloured pearls and Swarovski crystals to the bodice. It was now absolute perfection. It took my breath away, and I could not wait for Cade to see me in it.

I shivered in anticipation of my wedding in the next few days because, in about forty-eight hours, I would become Mrs Cade Raine. It had such a lovely ring to it. That thought reminded me, I needed to collect my engagement ring from the jeweller where it was being cleaned and polished.

The day after Cade proposed to me, he arrived home from work and unceremoniously presented me with a small, black, velvet box. I opened it slowly, looking with wide-eyed wonder at the lovely ring nestled inside.

A large, champagne-coloured diamond was cradled in a flower-shaped setting of gold. On either side of the centrepiece, leaves curled upward, clinging to the band encrusted with tiny emeralds. I gasped at the beauty of the piece and almost dropped it.

In an instant, Cade caught the box, removed the ring, and dropped down onto one knee. Taking my left hand in his, my husband-to-be expertly slipped the floral masterpiece onto my ring finger and gently kissed the back of my hand.

"Now, it's official. We are engaged," he announced. As he stood up, he pulled me into his arms and kissed me intensely, before casually saying, "I hope you like the ring."

"Oh, Cade," I said breathlessly, with a tear rolling down my cheek, "I adore it."

"I'm glad you are pleased and that it fits you so well. It was my grandmother's, a family heirloom. Now, it's yours, with my promise to love you forever."

I could not stop smiling through my tears and clung to him for all I was worth. My heart was almost bursting with love for my fiancé.

Cade swept me up into his arms and carried me to the bedroom, where we made love all night long. It was only the next day that I realised we had not even had supper.

I was ravenous when I awoke and hoping to share breakfast with Cade, went to look for him, but he had already left for work.

I was enraptured by the exquisite ring on my finger. Even so, a small cloud of sadness came over me, as I realised that there was no one I could even go and show it to. I thought about sending a photo to my sister's cell phone. However, I knew she would then ask endless questions about the wedding and I couldn't bear to tell her she was not invited.

A sudden noise downstairs startled me out of my reverie. It sounded like Cade was still around, so I went to find him to hear if he would like something to eat.

When I got there, I noticed he was dressed and ready to leave.

Kissing him on the cheek, I asked, "Honey, don't you want to have something to eat before you go?"

"No, thank you, my Love. I have a few things I need to sort out this morning, and I want to get done quickly. I plan to be home around noon, so we can make sure everything is ready and leave early for the airport." He kissed me on my forehead and breezed out of the door.

I was still standing lost in thought when I heard the powerful engine of his sports car roar to life and ease out of the garage. When I could no longer hear the car driving away, I got out the checklist of things I needed to do that morning.

After collecting my engagement ring, I picked up the wedding gift I had bought for Cade from the engravers. Not having had much time the previous week, I was hard-pressed to think of something to buy a man who had everything.

I decided to get him a set of very expensive oil painting brushes, made of hog bristles, for large areas of painting, and sable hairs from the weasel for detailed work. I found the ideal copper tin to hold the brushes in and on the lid, I had the words engraved, 'Darling Cade. Paint the future with love. Amber xo' and the date we were to be married.

Realising there was still much to be done, I quickly finished my breakfast, and after washing a few dishes and making the bed, I dressed and dashed into town to run my errands.

When I returned home, I tidied up the house, thinking Cade would not be happy if we went away and left it in a mess. Then I finished my packing, before having a quick shower and putting on my travelling clothes.

It was almost noon when I heard Cade's Ferrari racing up the road.

He walked in the front door, and I flung my arms around his neck, giving him a big hug, kissing him on the neck, and giggling happily.

Appearing a little irritated, Cade pushed me away and said, "We will have plenty of time for that on honeymoon, Amber. Right now, I need to finish packing, shower, and change. The driver is going to be here to pick us up at one o'clock."

I felt momentarily disheartened at being rebuffed by my fiancé on such a happy day, but I rapidly shook off the unpleasant thoughts and feelings. There were so many wonderful things to look forward to; nothing was going to get me down.

Skimming through my checklist one last time, I was satisfied that everything was done, then I deliberately centred my thoughts on the fact that very shortly, we would be starting the journey of a lifetime.

It felt as if mere moments had passed since Cade arrived home when I heard him striding past the kitchen, into the entrance hall, pulling his suitcase behind him.

"I am quickly putting the Ferrari in the garage," he told me.

"Okay, my Love. I must just collect personal items, and I'm ready to go."

The front door clicked shut.

I went to the bedroom, picked up my handbag from the dresser, and returned to wait for Cade.

Right on cue, as he entered the kitchen and locked the inter-leading door to the garage, a horn honked outside.

Cade grabbed our two suitcases, one in each hand, and headed out the front door. Charles, the limousine driver, took the bags and popped them into the boot. Then, Cade collected his hand luggage, locked the front door, and the two of us climbed into the Mercedes Benz stretch limo.

The trip to Cape Town International Airport would only take about thirty minutes with no traffic delays.

As the luxury vehicle eased smoothly down the road, Cade expertly popped open the bottle of Dom Pérignon Champagne, which had been chilling on ice and poured us both a generous amount. Smiling, he lightly clinked his glass against mine. "To a wonderful wedding and an even more amazing honeymoon, my beautiful bride-to-be."

Grinning back joyfully, I replied, "I cannot wait to become Mrs Cade Raine. I will love you forever." We sipped our champagne; then I leaned forward to kiss him on his sensuous mouth, which tasted sweet and fruity.

We were both breathless when we pulled apart from that kiss. After properly composing ourselves, we continued to chat and giggle like high school teenagers, hardly noticing the passing of time on the drive to the airport.

The traffic flowed smoothly, and within half an hour, we were at the airport. Once we finished booking in for our flight, we made our way to the SAA Business Class lounge, where we had time for a relaxing lunch, coffee, and dessert.

While Cade confirmed the rest of our flights and itinerary, I read a magazine, while indulging in some sweet treats from the delightful choice of handmade chocolates. At some point, I must have dozed off, because the next thing I knew, Cade was shaking me awake, telling me that it was time to board our plane for Johannesburg.

Chapter 10

It was a two-hour flight from Cape Town to Johannesburg, where we had a brief stop before our international leg to JFK Airport in New York. We had just over sixty minutes to take a wander through the duty-free shops at OR Tambo International Airport, before we had to board the plane for America.

Shortly after boarding our USA flight, Cade and I were comfortably seated, in our business class seats. I was still feeling somewhat drowsy from my earlier snooze in the lounge, and fell asleep before the plane took off, not even bothering to recline my seat. I must have been tired, because the next time I awoke, we were over the Atlantic Ocean, or The Pond, as some folk are fond of calling it. I was still sitting bolt upright in my chair, with my head lolling forward uncomfortably.

Absentmindedly rubbing my aching neck, I spoke sleepily, "Hi, Cade. What did I miss?"

"Not much, Honey," he drawled. "It's nearly suppertime. Can I order you some coffee?"

"That would be lovely. I'll just go to the bathroom to freshen up."

I arrived back at my seat just as the evening meal was being served. It had been quite a few hours since we had lunch and I was famished. Menus were handed out while I was asleep, so Cade had ordered for both of us.

Supper was delicious. I was reasonably awake now, and we chatted about our travel itinerary and marriage arrangements. While I slept, he had looked at weather reports for the duration of our journey, and was somewhat apprehensive about stormy weather over the Pacific Ocean, which could cause some turbulence during the final leg of our flight to Honolulu.

I told him that I was more concerned about the weather for our wedding day and hoped that the storm would have passed by then. Cade seemed confident that it would be, according to the sites he had scanned on the weather in Hawaii.

After supper, we decided to get settled for the night and watch movies. I ordered a small glass of sherry, while Cade finished the wine from supper and while we watched our shows. I had chosen a romantic comedy, while he was enjoying an action film.

After all my napping, I did not feel tired at all. Cade, on the other hand, was exhausted by this time as only fifteen minutes into his movie, he was snoring peacefully.

I watched two movies before I felt sleepy again, but I eventually slept, because the flight attendant had to wake both of us for breakfast. The entire flight was sixteen hours long and only ninety minutes remained before landing at JFK. Just over an hour later, we barely had time to freshen up, before the seatbelt lights came on and we were making our descent down to the airport.

On our approach to the runway, we came in low over the water. I gazed intently out of the window and was able to see the buildings of New York, the shoreline and tiny cars, with people the size of ants. My first trip ever overseas. It was so thrilling to experience the pleasures of this journey.

Gathering all our belongings, I turned to Cade in great excitement and said, "New York, here we come."

He had booked us into the Ritz-Carlton Hotel for the night, to rest and recover from our long-haul flight from

South Africa, before embarking on the almost eleven-hour leg of our journey to Hawaii.

The hotel was a gorgeous place overlooking Central Park, and Cade made special arrangements for us to drop off our luggage, giving us the whole day to explore New York. I had never been to America, so I was an eager tourist.

What should have been a thirty-minute drive, turned into nearly sixty in peak hour traffic, but it was lovely to be chauffeur-driven because it gave us time to examine our surroundings. Cade had been to New York a few times, so he pointed out places of interest.

Once we left our luggage, we decided to stretch our legs by walking through Central Park. After all those hours in a confined space, it was great to be moving and breathing in the fresh spring air.

Central Park was more beautiful than I imagined. It was lush and green, with winding paths and stunning displays of flowers in bloom. We took a casual stroll, stopping to admire the view and take photographs along the way.

We arrived at The Loeb Boathouse, just as it was opening for brunch. We decided to stop and eat, before continuing with our walk. Central Park was also far more extensive than I had thought.

After our meal, we took a wander past Cherry Hill Fountain. I was feeling entirely overcome with happiness by this point and danced around like a giddy little girl at her first birthday party. After I collapsed laughing and panting into Cade's arms, he guided me to a bench, to sit for a minute. Then he suggested that we continue to the John Lennon Memorial, Strawberry Fields, and return to our hotel, where the chauffeur was waiting to drive us to Battery Park. Here, we met our tour guide at Castle Clinton, and from there, we caught the ferry to see the Statue of Liberty.

As we stood in front of the colossal Verdigris green statue, Cade and I solemnly read the words on the pedestal,

"I lift my lamp beside the golden door." A shiver went down my spine, as I absorbed these words inscribed on an icon of American history.

I was delighted to discover that our tour included access to Lady Liberty's crown. However, I was not quite prepared for the 377 steps up a spiral staircase to the crown platform from the main lobby. We had to stop a few times on our upward journey, so I could catch my breath.

Due to time constraints, we were unable to visit Ellis Island, but I filed it away as something to do on my next trip to New York.

The round-trip took about three hours and was very memorable indeed. By this time, we were feeling the effects of the long period of travelling, and went back to our hotel for an afternoon nap.

After we awoke, there was just enough time to shower and change before dinner at the Auden Bistro and Bar. We had reserved seating for the pre-theatre dining. After a tasty meal, it was time to head off to the Neil Simon Theatre, to watch the Broadway show, Cats. What an incredible experience. I was utterly enthralled from beginning to end, and another little shiver went down my spine as the realisation dawned on me: this was now my life. We finished the evening with post-theatre cocktails back at the Auden Bistro, accompanied by the culinary treat of a "flight of chocolate truffles" called Magic Carpet.

When we collapsed into bed that night, my mind was filled with pleasant thoughts about our dreamlike time, and as I drifted off to sleep, I pictured the delightful days that lay before us. Our island destination wedding and honeymoon, as well as spending the rest of my life with an amazing man. Bliss…

Chapter 11

We were awake early the next morning, as our flight was leaving at ten, and even though we left the hotel at six o'clock for JFK, traffic was busy, and it took over an hour to get there.

For the first time since meeting Cade, I truly began to understand just how easily things were taken care of when money paved the way. We had checked in online and dropping off our luggage was a cinch. We were travelling in Premium Cabin class on Hawaiian Airlines and had free access to the Terminal Five Airspace Lounge.

While we were waiting to catch our flight, I noticed that Cade was still a bit agitated about the weather on this next leg of our trip. I tried to reassure him, by saying I was certain the airline would not risk flying in bad weather.

When we boarded the plane, we were offered complimentary drinks, which included a glass of Prosecco or a Mai Tai. It seemed a little early to be drinking alcohol, although I could see Cade was tempted. I decided to err on the side of caution and chose the pineapple juice. My husband-to-be elected to have a glass of Prosecco.

Cade relaxed slightly once in the air, reading the newspaper and sipping his drink. I paged through the on-board magazine and watched a documentary. There was still thick cloud about, making it impossible to see the land below and hard to guess if it was rain or shine; a somewhat eerie feeling, as if the plane was drifting through cotton candy.

After lunch, the flight attendant had barely cleared our food trays away, when the seatbelt sign went on to buckle up. Apparently, we were heading straight into the bad weather Cade had been worried about. I felt him tensing up next to me.

The clouds became dark and ominous, and I could see flashes of lightning outside the window. Each time I saw it, I jumped with fright and grabbed Cade's hand. He closed the window shade in the hope I would be less edgy. The flight was becoming very bumpy indeed, as we hit air pockets, causing severe turbulence.

After what seemed to be an interminable time, during which I felt as if I was barely breathing, the storm cleared, and we were once more on an even keel. Cabin service was resumed, and Cade ordered us each a cup of coffee, although I am sure he would have preferred a stiff drink. As it turned out, the pilot was one of Cade's schoolmates and a huge admirer of his art, so he was invited to go and visit in the cockpit. This practice is no longer common these days, due to security risks, but Cade was chuffed to see his old pal. I was left alone to amuse myself.

A couple of hours later, the seatbelt signs went on again. We had hit another storm, and although they were trying to fly above it, we experienced turmoil nonetheless. The aircraft dipped and bucked wildly, tossed about by the heavy wind. Regardless of size, no jetliner is a match for the forces of nature. I began to feel anxious and tried to get the flight attendant's attention, but at that moment, I saw she was taking care of another passenger, who had become air-sick.

I sat in my chair gripping the armrests for all I was wort, a wave of nausea welled up, and I thought I was going to retch. I closed my eyes, taking deep breaths, trying to quell my rising panic, and a sense of foreboding came over me. In an instant, despite the captain's instructions to remain seated and belted in, I had the incredible urge to find Cade. I needed him to sit with me, so I was not alone in the crazy storm. I managed to wait for what felt like a lull, before standing up. Just as I left my seat, the plane dropped abruptly, and I was flung up into the air like a ragdoll. As I came down, I must have hit my head on the armrest because I was knocked out cold.

My head pounded painfully, and my brain felt as if it was in a thick fog. I struggled to open my eyes. In the far distance, I could hear Cade calling me.

"Amber! Amber, please wake up."

My eyes opened gradually, and I found myself cradled in Cade's arms, his face just above mine.

A look of relief came over him as he hugged me close to his chest. I felt safe again.

It was in this vulnerable position that I was introduced to Cade's pilot friend, Mark. Both had rushed to my side after being called by the flight attendant, and between the two, they had lifted me carefully from the floor and placed me back in my seat.

Mark suggested the attendant bring me a cup of sweet coffee and a headache pill, as there was a noteworthy bump at the base of my skull, which throbbed agonisingly. He also told Cade to watch me for signs of concussion. I was not to sleep and if I felt nauseous or vomited, Cade was to call for immediate aid.

Cade very kindly held a cool cloth over the swelling while I drank my coffee. After a time, the wicked throbbing ease and I lay back in my seat with my head cradled comfortably against a soft cushion. My eyes just wanted to close, but Cade squeezed my hand and kept talking to me, waking me, and getting my attention, whenever I started to drift off.

I felt a great deal better by the time we landed at Daniel K Inouye International Airport, Honolulu, but Cade said he was not taking any chances and found a driver to take us straight to emergency, at The Queen's Medical Centre.

Once I was examined by the doctor and given the all-clear, both Cade and I were reassured. Even the inflammation had reduced significantly, and the discomfort was minimal. We heaved a sigh of relief and rushed off to catch our flight to the Four Seasons Resort, Lanai, where we were getting married the next day.

Hawaiian Airlines were very accommodating under the circumstances and managed to get us onto an alternative flight to Lanai Airport. The trip was only half an hour long, and we were barely off the ground when we were once more, ready to land.

Thankfully, Cade had yet again arranged for a chauffeur to collect us from the airport to drive the twenty or so minutes to our destination. Although we had travelled in style, first class, and luxury all the way, I was exceedingly grateful to finally be situated in my beautiful ocean-view suite at the Four Seasons.

Chapter 12

The day dawned crisp and clear, with a mild breeze wafting in from the ocean. I stood on the balcony outside my bedroom gazing out at the horizon. It was perfect, just the way my life was going to be with Cade. Excitement ran through me, and I could feel a few butterflies fluttering in my stomach. 'Today is my wedding day!' I thought. 'I feel so blessed. What a gorgeous day, absolutely flawless.'

Turning back towards my room, I did a little happy dance, twirling around on my toes with arms outstretched. My feelings for Cade were soaring to new heights. In no time at all, I was ready to start all the activities that would fill my day and help me prepare for the nuptials later in the evening.

Just then there was a discreet knock on the door. A waitress had brought me a lovely breakfast, which I asked her to set out on the private lanai.

Gathering my notes and checklists, I went outside and sat at the small table, munching happily and looking across the stunning vista of the gorgeous Hulopoe Bay. Staring out at the azure blue ocean, I hoped to catch sight of spinner dolphins. To my great surprise and delight, a small pod leapt out of the water, in a playful, synchronised display.

The hotel was set among beautiful gardens, complete with waving palm trees, verdant green lawns, and stunning tropical flowers. Although I could not see them from where I stood, I knew the resort hosted two lovely swimming pools, one of which boasted a cascading natural-rock waterfall.

The phone in my suite rang and I quickly went indoors.

It was Cade. "Good morning, Beautiful. How is your head feeling today?"

"Much better, my Love. Hardly any pain at all and the swelling has reduced significantly."

"That is good news, Honey. So, you slept well?"

"I had a restful night. Those painkillers practically knocked me out."

"I hope you enjoyed the breakfast I ordered for you and I will see you later on the beach."

"I did indeed. Thank you for your thoughtfulness, Cade. I cannot wait to become your wife. I love you."

"I love you too, Honey. Bye." Cade blew a kiss into the receiver and ended the call.

I placed the phone back on the cradle and stared musingly out of the window. With a start, I noticed the time and realised it was running away from me.

I quickly scanned the items to be taken care of for the day. The Four Seasons boasted a fantastic spa and in a couple of hours was my first appointment for a massage and facial. Then I went on to the manicurist, followed by the hairdresser, and beautician for make-up.

It was many hours later, when I emerged from the beauty salon, feeling glamorously coiffed and pampered. My hair hung in soft curls, with a section smoothly clipped back on either side of my face, and a feathered fringe brushed to one side. Make-up was perfect and natural, and the nail technician had given me a fresh-looking, French manicure.

Eventually, I made my way back to my suite to get dressed. On my way, I stopped at reception to pick up my bouquet, which consisted of Strelitzias and Frangipani, interspersed with stems of cream and champagne-coloured pearls. The arrangement matched the circle of Frangipani flowers that would adorn my hair. The hairdresser had attached the bridal veil to the headdress, which flowed over my arm as I made my way through the lobby and up the elevator to my floor.

Since our phone call in the morning, I wondered what Cade was doing. After supper together the night before, Cade had accompanied me to my room and then retired to his own suite. We agreed not to see each other before the wedding. He had arrangements to finalise and I had preparations to make before we exchanged our vows. The next time I saw him, would be in the evening on the beach for our ceremony. I felt a little lost without him and could not wait to be together again. I was so looking forward to enjoying our honeymoon in this beautiful place.

Once I got back to my Ocean View Suite, I quickly went over my list, to ensure I had remembered everything, and realised that I had forgotten to pick up my earrings from the jeweller. During our delightful dinner the previous evening, Cade pulled out a small red box from his pocket and presented it to me with a flourish.

I grinned mischievously and handed him my gift. "Please open mine first, I don't get to surprise you very often."

Cade graciously accepted the parcel and proceeded to quickly unwrap it. There was a genuine look of pleasure on his face when he saw the especially selected paintbrushes in their engraved copper tin. He was delighted. "I will treasure these always, Amber, and think of you every time I use them to paint. Now it's your turn to open a gift."

I lifted the lid of the box he had given me to reveal a stunning pair of teardrop pearl and diamond earrings. He said his mother had hoped he would present them to his bride as the 'something old' to wear on her wedding day. I got quite choked up with emotion.

Cade tenderly wiped the tears from my eyes with his thumbs and gave me a quick, chaste kiss. We finished our meal and then my husband-to-be walked with me to my suite.

"Goodnight, my Love. Sleep well. I will see you tomorrow on the beach." He turned on his heels and walked away down the corridor.

Upon further inspection of the earrings in my room, I noted they looked very expensive, but also a little dull and could do with a good cleaning. I dropped them off at the jeweller in the morning on my way to the spa. As I was contemplating my next plan of action, there was another knock at the door.

My heart leapt, thinking it might be Cade, eager to see me, as I was to see him. I almost ran to the door and flung it open. To my surprise, it was a bellhop holding out a silver tray with a pretty gold bag perched on top. The jeweller had kindly sent the earrings up to my room.

Finally, it was time to get dressed. I made a quick call to the concierge to ask him to send one of the hotel staff upstairs, as previously agreed upon. Because I was alone in the suite, I could not manage to zip up the wedding dress or arrange the veil by myself.

A few minutes later, there was a third knock at the door, which revealed a uniformed maid. "My name is Lanea. I am here to assist you."

"Hello," I replied. "Please come in."

Lanea helped me get into my simple but elegant gown. Before she tied the sash around my waist and knotted it at the back, I checked the blue embroidery on the inside, recording the date of our wedding. I put on the pearl earrings, and Lanea clasped closed the matching necklace. Lastly, I picked up the gorgeous halo of Frangipani and placed it carefully on my head.

Lanea clipped it into place and arranged the veil attractively down my back. "Oh, Ma'am, you look so beautiful!" she said, tears glistening in her near-black eyes.

I smiled gratefully. "Thank you, Lanea. Please, will you carry my bouquet downstairs?"

"Certainly, Ma'am. It would be my pleasure." Lanea offered a small bobbed curtsey.

Just then, there was yet another knock at the door. Lanea went to answer it, while I wondered who it could be this time.

She returned carrying a small silver tray, which held an envelope bearing my name, and a black velvet box.

I quickly read the card, which was from Cade, 'Your something new, my love. Cannot wait to make you my wife. Cade xo.'

Inside was a stylish pearl and diamond brooch, in the shape of two butterflies, which I asked Lanea to pin onto the front of my sash.

Then I slipped on my gold ballet pumps and spun around in front of the full-length mirror. As the skirt flared out around me, I gave myself one last head-to-toe check. I looked and felt very much the bride.

"Let's go, Lanea," I said, as I almost skipped to the door, and threw one more glance around the room, to check that all my things were packed and ready to go. The hotel would move my suitcases to our honeymoon suite during the wedding.

Lanea and I climbed into the elevator and went down to the lobby. I thanked her once more and took my bouquet, before making my way out into the garden and down the flower-lined pathway that led to the beach.

I turned the corner and saw to my amazement, out on the sand, a beautiful archway covered in Strelitzias, Frangipani, and cream and gold ribbons. In front of that, was a square gold mat and carpet runner, lined with Frangipani flowers. Standing to the right of the rug, was the most handsome man I had ever seen.

Cade was dressed in an immaculate beige suit, with matching casual loafers and a pale silk shirt, the top buttons open to reveal his bronzed throat and gold pendant hanging around his neck. His blond hair gleamed like burnished brass in the light of the setting sun, and his ice-blue eyes sparkled, as he smiled at me.

At that moment, I wanted to fly into his arms, but hesitated, briefly overcome with sadness, that there were no other loved ones present. No friends. No family. The only other people standing with Cade were the minister and the hotel manager, who, together with his assistant, had agreed to act as witnesses.

I shook the thought out of my head and ran to join my beloved. He held out both his hands and kissed me affectionately on the forehead, as I tightly clutched my bouquet. Then we stood side-by-side, gazing at the turquoise-blue water, with white sea-foam horses, breaking on the shore. Melodious strains of Hawaiian music floated on the pleasant breeze from somewhere in the hotel. We made our marriage vows, promising to love one another until death parted us. As if concurring, the setting sun slipped below the horizon in a spectacular display of yellow, orange, and red hues.

After exchanging rings, the minister said, "I now pronounce you husband and wife. You may kiss the bride."

Cade lowered his head to kiss me and whispered, "I love you, Mrs Raine."

Before I could reply, he pulled me hard against his chest and kissed me until I could not breathe. I told him, laughing, "You are squeezing me too tight, Mr Raine. I can hardly catch my breath."

"You are all mine now," he replied. "I want to hug you tight, and never let go."

I smiled, took his hand in mine, and motioned towards the photographer waiting for us to pose before the light completely disappeared. Kicking off our shoes, we ran down the shoreline and splashed in the waves. We stood with our arms wrapped around one another, kissing passionately. My dress got wet and I did not even care.

Tired but blissful, we went to sit down at our attractively laid out dinner table. My bridal bouquet had been placed in the middle as a centrepiece.

Sparkling wine lay chilling in an ice-filled champagne bucket. Cade poured us each a glass, and clinking them together, we offered one another tender toasts for a married life full of love and happiness. By the time we ate dinner, the wine was finished, and Cade ordered another bottle. I didn't think it was necessary, because I was not going to drink anymore, but it was our wedding night, and Cade was free to enjoy the delightful beverage.

Before dessert was served, Cade reached for my hand and asked, "Would you like to dance, my lady?"

I just smiled and stood up in response.

He swept me up into his arms and danced with me on the beach. That was the most romantic and perfect evening of my entire life.

Then, dessert was served, followed by a cheese plate. When we finished our lovely dinner, I was surprised to note that Cade had polished off the entire second bottle of wine all by himself.

Without thinking, I admonished him, "Cade, don't you think you've had too much to drink?"

To my utter astonishment, he leapt up, knocked over the chair, and slammed his hands down on the table.

Positioning his face frighteningly close to mine, he yelled at the top of his voice, "DON'T tell me what to do! Ever!!" He took his champagne flute, hurled it into the ice bucket, where it shattered into shards, and walked away.

I sat frozen in my chair, absolutely stunned and shocked at the unexpected behaviour. He had never acted like this before. After a few seconds, I gathered myself together and ran after him. I tried to follow in the dark, but he disappeared and did not reply when I called out to him. After wandering around for a while, it occurred to me that he might have gone back to the hotel. I gathered my shoes and bouquet, apologising profusely to the wait staff and made my way as quickly as I could to the Alii Royal suite.

I checked the lounge and outdoor lanai. He was not there. I also looked in the bedroom and en-suite bathroom. They were empty.

Utterly bereft, I collapsed in a heap onto the bed, sobbing, and hoped that he would return soon after he sobered up and came to his senses. Maybe we could talk and fix this, and our honeymoon would still be everything I dreamed.

Chapter 13

A ray of sunlight kissed my eyelids, and I awoke with a start, to discover that it was morning. I had fallen asleep on the huge king-size bed in my wedding dress. I instantly recalled lying there, waiting for Cade to return, feeling entirely alone, and devastated.

There was a damp spot on the comforter, under my left cheek. Still wet from the tears I had shed in my anguish and confusion during the night.

Our wedding night and he had stormed off in a temper. I did not know where he had gone even though I had searched for him, but all in vain. Then I decided I didn't want to upset him even further by not being in our suite if he came to find me. I cried and sobbed for hours and eventually fell asleep from sheer exhaustion.

Dragging myself from the bed, I removed my tatty veil and forlorn floral headpiece, hanging it behind the bathroom door. A glance in the mirror revealed panda-eyes, where my mascara had run and smudged into my make-up, forming black painted circles. My skin and lips were pale and streaked, where salty tears had trickled down my cheeks.

Then I carefully took off my gorgeous gown, which now looked more like a wet dishrag, and hung it on the hook with my veil. I stripped off my sexy underwear and staggered wearily over to the shower, turned on the taps, and stepped under the steamy hot spray. After rinsing my face and soaping down my body, I stood for a long time under the pouring water, letting it wash away my angst, and the fresh tears that were freely flowing.

After turning off the shower, I wrapped myself in the hotel bath sheet and wandered slowly back into the bedroom. I was still in a state of shock, having no idea what to do. Like an automaton, I dried, dressed, and fixed my hair, but did not bother to put on make-up. Nothing was going to hide my red, puffy eyes. I packed all my things and checked to make sure that I had left nothing behind. Not really having a plan, all I could think to do, was get a ride to the airport and fly home.

Cade wasn't coming back; I felt sure of it. He must have changed his mind about being married to me. If that was not the case, then he would have returned by now, and we could have talked about things. But he had chosen to stay away, and it could only point to one thing, he was done with me.

As I was about to leave, I heard a noise at the door. I turned around, just in time to see the handle turning, and in walked Cade.

His hair was a mess, his suit dishevelled, and his face taut and miserable. It appeared that he too could have been crying. I had never seen him like this. He carried in his hands a single red rose. My heart skipped a beat.

He strode deliberately towards me, dropped onto one knee in front of me and held out the rose like a sacrificial offering. Tears welled up in his eyes. "Amber, my love, can you ever forgive me?" he asked in a solemn tone.

I stood stiffly, my hands at my sides and whispered hoarsely, my throat raw from the night of sobbing, "What happened, Cade? Why did you react that way and leave me all alone on the beach on our wedding night?"

"I don't know, my Darling. I guess I had too much to drink. After I left you, I felt sick and dizzy, and I must have passed out, because I woke up early this morning lying behind a dune. My mouth felt dry and gritty, and my head was pounding so hard I could barely think," he offered hesitantly. "I sat on the sand trying to orientate myself until I recollected what had taken place, and then felt dreadful. Not knowing what you were thinking or feeling, all I knew was that I had to find you and apologise for acting so pathetically on the first night of our married life together."

Incredulously, I asked, "You were so drunk you passed out on the beach?"

"Yes," he replied. "I have no idea what came over me, I don't usually drink that much. You know me, I never have more than the occasional glass of wine. I got carried away. I am so sorry, Amber, please forgive me and let's start over. I promise that will never happen again. Please… Please, I'm begging you. I love you so much."

My heart melted, and I knelt before him, pulling him into my arms until his head rested against my bosom. I felt his warm tears falling on my breasts, and in an instant, everything changed.

Cade pulled me close and kissed me tenderly, and I felt the usual thrill of anticipation flow through my body. He lowered me down onto the thick pile of the luxurious carpet and began to kiss my eyes, earlobe, and the curve of my neck. His hands began to wander purposefully down over my hip and across my leg to the inner thigh. Just as his mouth reached my breasts, he pulled away from me.

Startled, I looked up at him with apprehension. But he proceeded to quickly remove his clothes and help me get out of mine. Naked we lay skin to skin, entwined in each other's arms and he made sweet, sweet love to me all day long. Afterwards, we lay comfortably relaxed in each other's arms, revelling in the afterglow of passionate lovemaking. I smiled to myself. This was how I had imagined our first night would be.

Upon reflection, the hurt of the day before still stung a little, but I decided to put it behind us and move forward. Cade had never behaved like this before, and now that he had apologised, I was not going to hold it against him. He seemed to be in a great mood and I did not want to spoil another single day.

The rest of our honeymoon was like a dream come true. We spent ten glorious days, soaking up the sun and swimming in the hotel swimming pools, as well as the ocean, where we also did snorkelling, kayaking, and sailing. It became more than obvious, Cade loved the sea and would have enjoyed scuba diving through the cathedrals. However, he was not going to be able to that on this occasion.

There was a trip back to Lanai to explore the village and local markets. Cade hired a dune buggy one day, and we had quite an exciting time racing across the island's rugged terrain. We went to look at the horses, but I did not know how to ride, so we also shelved that experience for another time. One of the most memorable moments, was when we hiked up to nearby Puupehe or Sweetheart Rock, as it's also known.

Cade and I stood atop Puupehe Rock arms folded comfortably around each other. He kissed the top of my hair and then lowered his head to kiss me full on the mouth. I sighed with pleasure, as we looked out over the view before us.

"Are you happy Mrs Raine?" he asked me.

"Yes, I am very happy indeed." I responded.

"Even though we got off to a rather rocky start?"

"Absolutely. You have more than made up for that first awful night. This honeymoon has been even more amazing than I could ever have imagined."

"Still want to be married to me forever?"

"Of course I do, silly. I am committed to you till death do us part."

Cade pulled me close and kissed me again, before we made our way, hand in hand, back to the hotel.

The second highlight was the helicopter flip over the ocean and around the island. We made a couple of close passes to view the shipwreck off the north-east coastline. The aerial views of this part of Hawaii were spectacular.

Flying in a big aircraft had not scared me, but I felt a little queasy in the small helicopter. A good excuse to wrap my arms around my hubby and hang onto him for dear life.

We ate our meals at a variety of charming restaurants, such as One Forty, Malibu Farm, and Nobu Lani. The food was wonderful and very different to home. I so enjoyed getting dressed up every evening and wait excitedly to see where Cade was taking me each night. The music and evening entertainment were sublime. It was almost surreal to be swaying to lilting island tunes in the arms of my loving husband and dancing cheek to cheek until the small hours of the morning.

This was the trip of a lifetime and, apart from our first awful night as a married couple, it was also idyllic. I managed to push that experience to the back of my mind, convincing myself that every newly-wed couple has differences and a disagreement or two at one time or another is quite typical. I felt safe and cheerful once more and Cade did not drink excessively again for the rest of our vacation.

There was only one other minor hiccup to mar our otherwise perfect honeymoon, and it took place the day we were to leave. While I completed the last of my packing, Cade went down to the beach for a walk. Once I finished, I went to join him. As I approached, I saw him standing near the water staring inscrutably at the horizon. A strange shiver passed through my body because as I regarded him, he looked morose and brooding. There seemed to be a dark aura surrounding him. I paused in my tracks, a sick feeling seizing me.

Cade turned my way with a deeply furrowed brow, a mean scowl on his face. My stomach lurched, I wanted to turn and run. Then as he saw me, his countenance changed and broke into a smile. My misgivings lifted, he looked happy to see me, and I ran across the sand to meet him. He caught me in his arms and swung me around until I was giddy. I giggled with delight like a little girl at her birthday party, and we ran along the shoreline hand in hand.

Then it was time to leave for the airport and catch our flights home.

Chapter 14

Life settled into a routine. Gone was the crazy-in-love and be-damned-with-everything-else attitude we had before the wedding. After some lengthy discussions between Cade and me, it was agreed that I would return to University to finish my degree. I was getting bored at home with nothing to do, and it was lonely with Cade at work all day. I consulted with the Head of the Fine Arts Department and explained my absence by telling her about my whirlwind marriage. She agreed to allow me to continue since I had only missed a few weeks and had been performing well up until the day I dropped out.

Cade returned to painting and spending time at his art gallery in Cape Town. His prior exhibition had seen great success, and his oil paintings were in huge demand. He began to spend long hours, both day and night, working on commissioned artworks and we saw very little of each other for a time.

However, things were good between us and still very passionate. Even if Cade arrived home very late at night, or in the wee hours of the morning, we made love often. It was as if he could not get enough of me. Sometimes, I was tired, or occasionally not in the mood, but I was always happy to comply because I reminded myself that I was married to this gorgeous man and sex was the only real demand he made. Truthfully, it was also good to feel sexy and desirable.

In the days that followed our wedding and honeymoon, I would occasionally question Cade about the promised reception party with our friends and family, which we planned to have upon our return. There were varying excuses, ranging from work to his ailing mother, and eventually, I gave up asking. I just knew it was never going to happen.

I so badly wanted to meet his mother, although I had heard she had Alzheimer's, and probably hardly even knew Cade anymore, let alone anything about his new wife. Each time he went to visit her, and I asked to accompany him, he would say, "Maybe next time. Let me see how she is doing today; things did not go well the last time I saw her."

It hurt that I was not included in that part of Cade's life. I also wanted him to meet my family and tried to plan visits to White River to spend time with my sister, Crystal, and her family, but to no avail. There was always a pretext, either his Mom or work. And he did not want me to go and visit them either. In the first two years of our marriage, I tried to make plans to visit my sister a few times, but eventually, there were too many secrets and things were so complicated it would be near impossible to explain.

My brother, Lane, was still overseas working in different places. We Skyped occasionally, but we were never very close during our childhood years, so we did not communicate regularly. After a time, even that stopped, because it just became too challenging.

While continuing my studies at University, I enjoyed spending time with my friends but kept that existence completely separate from my married life. After a while, I kept it secret as well, because every time I socialised with "the gang," I encountered resistance from Cade if he was around when I arrived home. Even if he asked about my day, what I had been doing, and who I was with, I kept my answers vague and no longer admitted to spending time with my young friends. As it turned out, the next time I saw his dark side, was one evening when I returned home after spending an afternoon with them.

I always tried to make sure I was home before him, so that I could avoid any possible confrontation. Cade worked long days, leaving for the art gallery early in the morning and returning very late at night. When I questioned him about spending so much time there, he responded that he had his art studio there as well, so he worked on paintings before the gallery opened and after it closed. That sounded logical, and although I was not happy about him spending so much time away, I accepted it, the way most wives do.
On this particular evening, Cade arrived home early for whatever reason and was waiting for me. I did not realise he was there because I parked the car in the driveway and the house was in complete darkness. I entered through the front door and headed straight for the kitchen, switching on lights as I went. It seemed eerily quiet, but I shook off the strange feeling and began preparing the evening meal. Regardless of the time Cade came home, he always wanted something to eat.

I often ate early and left his food covered in the fridge. I decided to do something simple and settled on salmon steaks, with boiled new potatoes and a green salad. I was busy washing the vegetables, when I got a creepy feeling that someone was watching me. The hairs on the back of my neck stood up, and I had goose bumps all over.

Before I could start cooking, I heard my cell phone ringing in my handbag, which was on the counter by the door. I turned to answer the call and jumped with fright, screaming "Oh!"

Standing silently in the doorway was Cade, with an ominous glare on his face.

"Cade, Honey, I didn't know you were home." Nervously, I approached him, not liking the dark scowl I saw on his countenance.

"Where the hell have you been?" he growled.

I stopped in my tracks. "I ... I was at the University."

"All day? I thought you only had classes this morning."

I was stunned, I did not know he had any clue about my schedule. "Well," I said cautiously, "I did spend some time with my friends after class."

"And did I not tell you to drop those deadbeats?" he asked, his voice low and menacing, and took a step towards me.

I immediately backed away. Trying to put some space between us. "Yes, you did, but you have been working so much lately that I was lonely. I needed company, and you were not around. I didn't think there was any harm in it because you were at the gallery." I babbled frantically, also feeling annoyed, because… for goodness sake, I was not a child in need of scolding for mixing with the 'wrong friends'.

Without uttering another word, Cade strode towards me and lashed out with a back-handed fist across my face, lifting me off my feet with the force of the blow, and hurling me across the room and onto the floor. Before I could even react, he was towering over me, and I could smell the alcohol on his breath as he ranted and raved at me.

Winded from the fall, I could not talk back and put up my arm to ward him off.

He grabbed my wrist and hauled me off the floor. As he yanked me up, he twisted my arm, making me scream in agony, and I felt something snap. At that moment, he instantly dropped me back onto the floor, as if he had been scalded.

I grabbed my broken wrist with my other arm, cowering in the corner, crying and sobbing in pain.

Instantly regretful, he dropped down beside me on the floor. "Oh, no, Amber, what have I done? I am so sorry; I didn't mean to do that." He reached his hand towards me.

"Don't touch me! Don't touch me!" I shrieked, recoiling away from him. I cradled my limp, aching wrist with my good arm.

"I'm sorry, Amber," he said in a soothing tone.

Slowly kneeling beside me, he placed his hands lightly on my shoulders, feeling my violent tremors. His face was contrite, his voice soft, and sincere. "Amber, I am truly sorry. I did not mean to hurt you. Please forgive me. Let me take you to the hospital."

I merely nodded numbly, in too much agony, physically and emotionally to even speak. I meekly acquiesced, not wanting to set him off in a temper again.

With a surprising gentleness, he picked me up and carried me to his car. We drove in silence for a few minutes on our way to the hospital, broken only by an occasional sob from me. Cade continued apologising and begging for my forgiveness. We were both crying, and by the time we arrived, I was delirious with pain.

When the staff at the Emergency Room asked what happened, before I could respond, Cade told the admitting nurse that I fell down the stairs in our house. I guess that was an acceptable explanation, because nobody questioned me any further, despite the lack of evidence or bruising related to such a fall. I had a red welt on my cheek and perhaps that was enough to convince them. I decided to keep quiet about what Cade had done as well because I did not want to cause trouble or upset him again. And he seemed genuinely remorseful.

After what felt like an endless wait, I was sent for an x-ray, which confirmed a small bone in my wrist was fractured. The attending doctor set it in a cast, gave me a prescription for some strong analgesics and sent me home with my husband.

During the drive back, I was a little woozy from the painkillers. Cade was persistently apologetic and treated me so tenderly that I began to wonder if I had not imagined it all and had actually fallen down the stairs. He kept telling me over and over how much he loved me and begged for my forgiveness. I desperately wanted to believe him, so I pushed all misgivings out of my mind and complied.

Once we got home, Cade carried me into the house and placed me on the comfortable couch in the sitting room. He brought me a glass of water and tucked a throw around my legs. He even brought me a magazine to read, while he finished making the supper I had started earlier.

We ate quietly together and then he carried me to our room. He brought me my painkillers, and by the time he had finished showering and climbed into bed, I was sound asleep.

I woke up in the early hours of the morning with a stab of soreness in my wrist and the weight of a heavy body on top of me. About to scream, I realised it was Cade, making love to me while I slept. My mind was fuzzy from the drugs, and I could not entirely grasp what was going on. Inwardly, I felt panicked, but lay silent for a moment, trying to figure out what to do. If I was confrontational, he might get angry again, and it was so weird that he was doing this while I was in no state to participate. As I opened my mouth to speak, he climaxed, rolled off me, and strode naked through to the bathroom.

I noticed I was holding my breath, and when I heard the shower going, let out a long gasp of relief. My broken wrist was throbbing. I sat up in bed, fumbled about on my nightstand for the painkillers, and swallowed two more with a long draught of cold water. My breathing was rapid and shallow, my heart thumping in my chest. I lay back in bed and closed my eyes, praying that this was all just a bad dream.

When I awoke the next morning, I was in bed alone, but next to my glass of water was a small vase with a beautiful rose and a note from Cade. "Gone to work, my

Love, I will be home early tonight. Call me if you need anything and take it easy today."

I shook my head to clear the fog of sleep from my mind and mentally ran through what had occurred the day before. None of it made any sense, it felt like a bad dream—totally unreal, except for the genuine pain in my arm.

Cade called me a few times during the day, to check on how I was doing and if there was anything I needed. He did this throughout my convalescence, and I enjoyed the extra attention and tender loving care.

When he came home that first evening, he acted as if nothing was amiss, except for my broken wrist. He took care of me the way any loving husband would. He made meals, brought me tablets, and helped me to shower. This pattern became our daily routine until I recovered completely.

Naturally, my fractured arm healed in a few weeks, and the memories of that awful night began to fade. Life was peaceful and relaxed once more. So determined was I to make this marriage work and be content, that I firmly put all the fear and awful thoughts out of my mind. So, Cade had slipped up a couple of times, which did not make him a bad husband; in fact, maybe it was my fault. After all, he had reacted angrily to the things I said, so the blame was not on him, but apparently on me.

Chapter 15

I was in my final year of study towards my Degree when my twenty-first birthday approached. Cade and I had been together almost a year, and I thought it would be special if we had a joint party for our first wedding anniversary and my birthday.

I was not sure how to broach the subject since Cade did not want me spending time with my friends, but likewise, he did not socialise at all. This was a tricky situation. I decided to talk to him about it anyway, as we had never had the big reception I had hoped for after our wedding.

I knew Cade was taking time off from the art gallery to spend at home with me the following weekend, so I enthusiastically planned a picnic at the beach, just like the one we shared on our first date.

Saturday dawned bright and beautiful. I woke up and looked over at my sleeping husband. He truly was handsome, and I felt my heart go pitter-patter.

Just then, Cade opened his eyes to find me staring at him. "Hey, gorgeous. You're up early." He reached out with one of those bronzed muscular arms and pulled me towards him, my breasts pressing against his broad, hard chest. He kissed me deeply, passionately, and with a guttural groan rolled over on top of me and started making love with wild abandon.

We were lying cuddling, basking in the afterglow when I pitched the idea of a sunset picnic on the beach. He was enthusiastic about the notion, so after showering and dressing, I set about recreating the exact picnic basket that he had packed for me almost a year before.

To give me time to get it all together, Cade went into our home gym for his daily workout, which was usually followed by a long run through the neighbourhood. While he was gone, I decided to do some self-indulging. I wanted to make myself pretty for him.

By the time Cade returned, I was finished with the pampering and trying to figure out what to make for lunch. He did not feel like eating lunch, deciding instead to have a protein shake, so I made myself a sandwich and went to eat it in the garden, enjoying the sunny day.

Later, while he worked on one of his oil paintings, I started reading a new book I had bought. It was a lovely, tranquil day and I was looking forward to our outing.

It was late afternoon when Cade and I climbed into the car and drove down to Hout Bay beach. We walked hand in hand on the sand to the secluded spot where we had enjoyed our first picnic. Once more, we laid out a blanket and unpacked the basket.

There was the peach sparkling wine, cheese and crackers, fresh strawberries this time instead of cherries, and some mint chocolates. I had also remembered to pack the crystal champagne glasses and original cream and gold porcelain plates.

Cade looked delighted that I had almost perfectly duplicated our very first picnic and seemed very relaxed and in a great mood.

I, on the other hand, was biding my time, waiting rather impatiently until we finished, chatting about a variety of topics as a distraction. Sipping our second glass of bubbly, I broached the subject of a party, beginning tentatively, "Cade, you know that we never had the big wedding party we planned after our honeymoon?"

"Yes, Amber, I do remember," he responded defensively. "We did not have the time for that after we got back from honeymoon. I became incredibly busy with the gallery and my commissions, and you went back to University."

Trying to appease him, I quickly continued, "I'm not harping. I merely brought up the subject because I wanted to talk to you about something related to that."

Cade's reply was terse. "Go on."

I laid my hand on his arm and felt him stiffen. I gazed at him beseechingly and stated my case. "I was thinking that with our first wedding anniversary coming up, and my twenty-first, we could have a big party and celebrate both occasions at once."

For a couple of minutes, Cade did not speak and looked tense.

I began to feel anxious, my mouth was dry, and my heart beating rapidly.

"Amber, I don't think we will be able to have a party." He spoke in measured tones.

My heart sank.

"I planned to surprise you. However, I don't want you to be upset, so I may as well tell you now. I've planned a cruise for us, to celebrate those two very special occasions."

"W…what?" I yelled with great excitement. "Where? When?" And just like that, all my misgivings flew out the window again.

Cade smiled. "I have booked us on an amazing cruise, starting on the day before our wedding anniversary, until the day after your birthday. We will fly to Barcelona, Spain, where we will board a luxury liner and travel around the Mediterranean for ten days."

"How wonderful! That sounds fantastic, Cade. I can hardly wait."

He looked very pleased with himself.

Even so, whereas this was a truly incredible trip and I was genuinely happy, I still felt sad that I was unable to invite my friends and family to celebrate our anniversary or my birthday. I admonished myself, to not be ungrateful, that not everyone had this kind of opportunity. There was plenty of time in the future for parties, and I knew that we would have many great times yet. I was determined to appreciate my husband's thoughtfulness and generosity.

Chapter 16

The days flew by and before long, Cade and I were headed for Spain. As usual, he spared no expense, and we travelled in style. We could take advantage of the first-class lounge before boarding and I longed to call my family or a friend to tell them my exciting news. But the barrage of unanswerable queries that would unleash kept me in check. Once on the plane, we enjoyed luxury, privacy, and comfort, being able to share a meal at a table for two, which was very romantic flying high above the clouds.

After a fourteen-hour flight, during which we were able to sleep on flat private beds, and a brief stopover in Zurich, we landed at Aeroport del Prat in Barcelona, Catalonia, feeling well-rested and ready for our adventure. As an additional bonus, we got to watch the sunrise from the plane before we landed.

As soon as we collected our luggage, Cade suggested we stop at a restaurant to have a leisurely breakfast, before taking a taxi to the Port of Barcelona to board the cruise ship, The Nautica.

As naïve as I was, not having travelled much, I had no idea that we were afforded a special privilege by being allowed aboard the ship at eleven in the morning. This was due to yet another wonderful surprise, as Cade had booked us an Owner's Suite, with its private veranda and ocean view. He also informed me that with these privileges came a twice-daily maid and twenty-four-hour butler service. I had never been so spoilt in my life! Just being on the ship was an experience, let alone all the wonderful places we were going to visit.

I was sorry we were not able to spend more time in Barcelona, but Cade assured me that he had booked us into a hotel for the day after our return from the cruise and we would then do some sightseeing before flying home.

Our suite on-board was fabulous, and after unpacking cases and taking an invigorating shower together, we went to explore the ship and enjoy a light lunch. Afterwards, I felt utterly exhausted from all the travelling and excitement, so we decided to take an afternoon nap in the queen-size Tranquility Bed.

I awoke refreshed, but alone in the bed.

Cade came wandering through with a towel wrapped around his waist and a big grin on his face. "How would you like to join me in the Jacuzzi, my Love?" he asked.

My reply was to leap off the bed, give him a big hug and run past him into the bathroom. I quickly hopped into the bubbling water before he could even turn around and follow me. We snuggled close to each other in the swirling warmth, sipping on chilled Champagne and sharing intimate kisses. It wasn't long before the fire of desire was ignited and we hurried back to the bedroom to make love.

Lying curled up in Cade's arms, feeling glad and content, I heard a knock on the door and quickly drew the bedcovers over my chest.

Cade gave me a brief smile and pulled on his bathrobe before going to answer. Our personal butler was waiting to serve us the in-suite dinner that Cade had ordered. He asked the man to return in about ten minutes, to give us time to get dressed.

When the butler returned, he presented us with a bowl of fresh fruit to start our meal and a light supper of grilled, honey-basted salmon and new potatoes with steamed broccoli. Dessert was one of my favourites, crème caramel.

After supper, we decided to take a stroll around the ship and wandered past a very up-market boutique, the casino, and various bars and lounges before stopping at an observation lounge, called Horizons, where there were dramatic floor-to-ceiling windows. I knew the daytime views would be spectacular. We decided to have a quick nightcap, before returning to our suite.

The following morning, we rose early to enjoy a delightful breakfast on our private veranda overlooking the ocean, before docking at the "Puerto de Valencia". It was the initial leg of our cruise, and I could not wait to explore.

Our first stop was the "Ciutat de les Arts i les Ciències" or City of Arts and Sciences, an entertainment-based cultural and architectural complex in the city of Valencia. The centrepiece building boasts a Laserium, called "L'Hemisfèric" also known as the "eye of knowledge". The entrance to the complex includes a landscaped walkway named "L'Umbracle". It features plant species indigenous to Valencia. Within, can be found "The Walk of the Sculptures", consisting of numerous figures surrounded by nature.

Cade and I had a great deal of fun, posing with the sculptures and taking selfies with our cell phones. It was certainly unique and enjoyable.

Having experienced a modern aspect of Valencia, we decided to find somewhere to have a light lunch and came across a restaurant en-route, called La Nicoletta, where we enjoyed house wine and tasty pizza.

Then, we made our way to the gothic style Valencia Cathedral. Beautiful carvings adorn the exterior of the main gate, but by far the most interesting section sculpturally is the "Apostles' Door", above which is the stained-glass rose window holding "The Star of King David." The interior is also ornately decorated and has several large paintings.

By now it was late afternoon, and we decided to return to the ship for sundowners and to get ready for our evening meal, which we were planning to eat in the "Toscana" restaurant.

Feeling somewhat daring that night, I dressed in a slinky, black, full-length dress. The halter-neck revealed a good bit of cleavage, and there was a deeply plunging 'V' at the back. This sexy outfit also had a side-seam slit designed to show off a hint of leg every now and then.

Cade's enthusiastic wolf-whistle upon seeing me in this gown, made my heart dance. He looked utterly gorgeous in a pale blue ensemble. It took great resolve to leave our suite and make our way to the restaurant, where they served Tuscan food on Versace china.

Afterwards, we went to listen to "classical music under the stars". We relaxed blissfully for an hour before retiring to our suite. It had been a busy day, and I was tired, but evidently, the dress I had chosen to wear for the evening had sparked my husband's yearnings. Not that I wanted to get out of love-making and it was the perfect end to a wonderful day.

Our next port of call was Palma de Mallorca in the Balearic Islands of Spain. We began our exploration of the island with a meander down Paseo Maritimo, a palm-lined boulevard that runs along the coast. Palma features a variety of local arts and crafts, so we decided it was time to do a little souvenir shopping. We stopped at a little stall that sold glass pendants, and Cade bought me one in a teardrop shape with a white almond blossom on a gold background. It hung from a white silk ribbon, which my husband fastened around my neck.

The favourite local dish is spicy Spanish pork loin or "Lomo Adobado". We chose a restaurant called Cellar SA Premsa which served another popular pork dish, loin with cabbage and a side dish of Tumbet, a mixture of eggplant, potatoes, zucchini, garlic, and tomato sauce.

We decided to walk off our food by visiting the Bellver Castle, which is another gothic-style building, on top of a hill, and a symbol of the city of Palma. One of the few circular castles in Europe, it was used for a couple of centuries as a military prison. Since coming under civilian control, it is now a popular tourist attraction and houses the city's history museum.

Before we returned to the ship, we tried another Mallorca favourite, Ensaimadas or traditional sweet bread which we dunked in our coffee. Then it was time to leave the island and board our luxurious floating hotel again.

We had a lovely day exploring the island, but I was excited for the night ahead. Cade and I were invited to dine at the Captain's table in "The Grand Dining Room", and we were going to dress up.

I had brought a gorgeous long evening gown in shimmering bronze to wear for this special occasion. My striking husband was decked out in his best tuxedo and was by far the most handsome man on the ship.

We were graciously received by the Captain before being seated at his table. We were introduced to the other guests who had been invited and the evening was filled with great conversation and some good laughs.

Dinner was just as delicious as we expected it to be, with a delightful cheese soufflé appetiser, followed by a baby spinach salad. The entrée was "Duck à l'Orange", accompanied by braised red cabbage and almond potato croquettes. I was famished when we started eating, but felt so full that I decided to forgo dessert, until I saw it was baked "Valrhona" chocolate cake with raspberries and vanilla ice cream and I could not resist. The meal was accompanied by French champagne, and afterwards, platters of cheese and biscuits were served with tea or coffee. The Captain was a charming and interesting man and the dinner table talk was lively and entertaining.

After a delightful dinner, Cade and I decided to return to the Horizons bar to dance the evening away. It was a great day, topped off with a lovely romantic night. I felt as if I was on cloud nine, swaying to the music in Cade's arms until the wee hours of the morning.

The next day was to be spent travelling at sea, across the Mediterranean, so we decided to sleep in a bit and have a late first meal, before doing some more exploration on the cruise liner.

Instead of eating in our room, which we had done the first couple of mornings, we decided to try another of the many restaurants aboard the ship and discovered the Terrace Café. We had a delightful breakfast and enjoyed watching the undulating ocean as we sipped our coffee.

We took a wander past the casino again, the beautiful shops, where we did some window shopping and ended up outdoors at the poolside. It was one of those beautiful, balmy days, reminiscent of Hawaii. We found a couple of loungers in a secluded spot and the two of us took turns slathering on the sunscreen, before toasting in the sun for a while.

By midday, it was getting quite hot, and we went for a swim in the lovely, cold pool. We swam and splashed about for a while, chasing each other through the water. Cade is a strong swimmer, his muscular arms cleave through the water, moving his body like a torpedo. However, not too shabby a swimmer myself, he did not always catch me as easily as he thought he would. But once we had tired of frolicking in the pool, we returned to our loungers to dry off and relax.

Later, after a light lunch at Waves, Cade and I decided to spend some time at the on-board spa. We started with a body conditioning "Ocean Scrub" and ended with a "Two-by-Two" aromatherapy massage.

Feeling very tranquil, we returned to our suite to shower and prepare for the evening. We were going to enjoy some cocktails in the Horizons observation lounge and watch the sunset before dinner.

In our suite, Cade opened the usual complimentary champagne bottle, and I took a glass with me into the

Jacuzzi. When I returned, Cade was not in our room, so I dressed, got myself ready, and went to sit on our private veranda. About to pour myself another glass of champagne, I realised the bottle was empty. A bit puzzled, I poured myself a sherry instead and went outside.

A temperate breeze lifted my hair, and I breathed in the salty scent of the ocean as I stood alongside the railing. Closing my eyes, I listened to the sound of the waves from the bow of the ship, standing for a long time, sipping my sherry. Eventually, it was getting quite dark, so I thought I should go inside and perhaps look for Cade.

As I turned around, there he was, his large frame filling the doorway. He said nothing, but he had this strange look on his face, and a small frisson of fear ran down my spine.

He moved quickly towards me, grabbed the sherry glass from my hand, and tossed it overboard. In the same movement, he pulled me roughly towards him, and I could smell the champagne on his breath.

"Cade, what's wrong?"

He pushed me so hard against the railing I thought I'd topple over into the sea. Terrified, I grabbed him, grasping handfuls of clothing.

He lowered his head and kissed me, hard…

I could not breathe. The taste and stench of alcohol made me gag.

Without saying a word, he picked me up in his arms and for a single moment, I imagined he was going to toss me overboard like the sherry glass. Instead, he turned, walked into our bedroom, and threw me onto the bed. The next second, he ripped off my clothes, climbed on top of me and began violently raping me.

There was no gentle kissing or tenderness. Only hard roughness and extreme agony as he pushed himself viciously into me. He held me pinned firmly with his hands on my arms against the bed and the weight of his legs on mine. I could feel his cruel fingers digging into my flesh as I cried out in pain.

He did not even look at me. His face was flushed crimson and contorted into a hideous monster, jaws wide open and panting like a rabid animal.

I was so stunned that I could not think of what to do, then I tried to get him off me, by heaving my body back and forth beneath his vice-like grip. "What are you doing?" I screamed, "Stop hurting me! Why are you doing this?"

He swiped at me viciously with a backhand across the face and shouted, "Shut up, you whore!" Then he rolled off me, pulled up his pants, and stormed out of our suite.

I lay there shocked and shaking all over, wondering what the hell had just happened and felt myself beginning to fill with rage. 'Bastard! How dare he?"

In our year of marriage, I never refused him sex. Why would he feel the need to violate me like that?

Gloria, who had been sitting quietly listening to my tale, came over and hugged me.

"Amber, rape is never about sex, it is about power and control. It also sounds to me like your husband cannot hold his liquor. It appears to have a detrimental effect on him."

"You're right, and in those early days, each time he abused me was after he had too much to drink. But it happened so rarely and unpredictably, that I was never prepared. Most of the time he would enjoy a single glass of wine. Then out of the blue, he would imbibe a bottle or two and turn into a vicious beast."

"Even so, that does not excuse his behaviour, it only makes it worse," interjected Gloria, "There must be something exceedingly broken within the man to ever act that way."

"There is something undeniably wrong with Cade."

Gloria pressed a tissue into Amber's hand and said soothingly, "I will make us another nice warm cuppa, and you can continue, if you feel up to it."

"Thank you, Gloria. That will be nice." Amber dried her eyes with the tissue and took a deep breath before continuing.

When I had calmed myself, I struggled to my feet. My body ached all over, and my legs trembled as I tried to walk. Fresh waves of fear and anger washed over me. I stumbled into the bathroom and took a long hot shower, scrubbing my skin repeatedly, as if I could remove the feel of Cade's violation with soap and a loofah.

In my mind, I went over the two previous occasions he had hurt me in the year since we married. Although he did not harm me on our wedding night, I now know that it was emotional abuse. I thought about the time he broke my wrist. That was unmistakably abuse, but it was still early days in our relationship, and I loved him. I did not want to think that my husband would ever intentionally hurt me to that extent.

Here I was, one year into marriage to this man and he had now sexually violated and physically injured me. I longed to shout out my torment and rage at him. I opened my mouth to howl, but no sound would come out. I just stood there, mouth wide open, unable to breathe, letting out a silent scream.

A long time passed before I turned off the water and wrapped myself in a towel to dry. Looking in the mirror, I saw yet again a swollen red welt on my cheek and bruises were starting to form on my upper arms, where his hands had gripped me so tightly. Turning away from these reminders of savagery, I threw on my nightgown and crawled into bed, where I curled up into a ball and cried for hours.

Each time exhaustion threatened to overcome me, I would be assailed by a fresh flood of tears and pummelled my pillow in resentment and frustration. I imagined that I was fighting back at my callous husband.

I did not manage to fall asleep and finally heard the suite door open. My heart thumped wildly in my chest, but I pretended to be sleeping, hoping Cade would leave me alone.

When he climbed into bed, I could once more smell the strong alcohol emanating from him; it was all I could do not to throw up. I lay there, as still as I could with my eyes shut, hardly daring to breathe. A few minutes later I heard him snoring soundly. Sometime later, I too fell asleep.

Chapter 17

The next morning, I awoke with an instant memory of the night before. I lay there rigid, eyes closed, my mind whirling with dreadful thoughts, trying to figure out how to handle the insane situation. I had been raped by my husband. It did not make any sense to me. We always had a passionate relationship, and I never denied him, why did he feel the need to take so violently what was already his?

I was physically and emotionally debased and sick with distress, lack of sleep, and continued anxiety. I did not know how to face this man, could not even bear to look at him.

When I felt Cade's hand on my arm, I froze, too scared to move for fear of what might follow, and my heart hammered out of control.

"Oh, Honey, I truly overdid it with the champagne last night. I have a thundering headache and awful hangover. Did you bring any headache pills with you?"

Astounded by the casual tone, I could hardly respond. "I… I did," I stammered. "They are in the bathroom cabinet; I'll get them quickly."

Before I could move, Cade replied, "Don't worry, I'll find them. Then I'm going to order breakfast, would you like some?"

"No thank you, I'm not hungry. I think I'll freshen up and get dressed."

"Okay," he said, completely unperturbed by my unusual lack of appetite.

Obviously, Cade did not recall what had transpired the night before, other than drinking the champagne. He did not even notice my pink, swollen cheek, from his blow to my face and mottled contusions on my arms. I decided to play it cool and not confront him about the rape, in case I provoked him to anger yet again.

I applied some foundation to my cheek to cover the marks and donned a blouse with sleeves, so as not to expose the bruises.

This was the day we were docking at Palermo, Sicily, and going ashore to do some exploration. I had been looking forward to another excursion, but now I felt fatigued, sore all over and extremely vulnerable, both physically and emotionally. Not to mention still upset over the whole incident and wary that this appalling side to my husband might show itself again at the slightest provocation.

Cade continued acting as if nothing had happened and once his headache was gone, he seemed very pleased and satisfied with himself, chatting pleasantly about what we were going to do and see.

Before we left, I took a couple of painkillers myself and resolved to enjoy the day despite what had happened the night before. We had been told that Palermo is a paradise for lovers of food and culture.

As we had done in the former cities visited, we went to see the Palermo Cathedral, which is dedicated to the belief that the Virgin Mary was physically welcomed into heaven. Some might say it is perhaps the best tourist attraction in Palermo, Sicily.

This building houses an earlier kind of solar observatory, or meridian heliometer. It is essentially a small hole in the roof of the dome, through which an image of the sun is projected across the floor at a time called "solar noon". Running north to south along the floor is a bronze line. At specific points on either side are images of "La Meridiana" or symbols of astrology. They indicate both the summer and winter solstice. A fascinating blend of Christianity and astrology. It also has a rich and varied history, including part of it being a mosque at one time.

Within the Cathedral is the Sacrament chapel, lavishly decorated with precious stones and lapis lazuli. As we walked through admiring the interior, I stopped for a moment and under my breath, offered up a quick prayer for Cade, myself, and our marriage. I knew now for certain that something was seriously wrong with him, but I didn't know what or how to deal with it. We both needed divine intervention.

As if sensing the hesitation in me, Cade stopped, and said, "Isn't it beautiful, Honey?"

"Yes, it is." I agreed enthusiastically. "I love the precious stone decorations, together with that unusual blue of the lapis lazuli."

My comments might have appeared a bit forced because he stopped and stared down at me rather enigmatically. Taking my arm, he guided me on to the Saint Rosalia Chapel, which was locked behind a gate made of bronze. Saint Rosalia was the patroness of Palermo. Her remains are contained in a silver box decorated with precious stones. She is, possibly, regarded even more highly than the Trinity and perhaps more than even the Virgin Mary. We spent a long time at the Cathedral, as it was an incredibly beautiful and interesting place to visit.

We decided to stop for an early lunch before continuing with our sightseeing. Since I had not eaten breakfast, I was now quite famished. At Trattoria Primavera, we ate pizza accompanied by the house wine.

"So, what do you think of our anniversary cruise so far, Amber?"

"It is absolutely lovely," I gushed. "These old cities and their attractions are just amazing. The ship is magnificent, and our suite is perfect. Thank you for this indulgence, Cade. I appreciate you spoiling me like this."

"It is a pleasure, my Love," replied Cade and kissed the back of my hand, reminding me of that first day we met on the beach in Hout Bay. A shiver passed through me, as I realised that the man I had married was not the one I thought I had met that day. I shook off the feeling of foreboding, as my husband was pulling me to my feet and we continued with our day trip through the city.

The "Fontana Pretoria" in the Piazza della Pretoria was our next stop. This spectacular fountain rotates around a central basin, surrounded by four bridges of stairways, and a railing fence. At the top is one statue pouring water, which falls into three elevated basins. Surrounding the lower three concentric pools are several naked monster and nymph effigies spraying water, that also caused it to be known as the "fountain of shame" at one time.

Cade asked me to take a photograph of him in front of this aptly named tourist attraction, completely oblivious to the incongruity of such a request. Certainly for me, after what had transpired the previous night.

Even more absurd at this point, was that my peculiar husband, in a romantic gesture, took my hand affectionately in his and proceeded to walk this way through the streets of the city. Looking convincingly like a couple in love to anyone who might notice. They would have to pay close attention to see the slight stiffening of my body when Cade kissed my cheek or forehead.

Continuing on our tour, the next stop was a baroque-style church called "Casa Professa" or Church of Saint Mary of Gesu, with ceiling frescoes and stained glass as well as marble carvings at the main entrance. It is ornately decorated with a lovely tiled floor. Appropriately, churches are a great pride for Palermo.

Once the outing was over, we returned to the ship. To my relief, Cade did not open the usual complimentary bottle of champagne but instead suggested a quick shower and an early dinner. Determined to keep the peace, I went along with his plans and we had a lovely evening.

The Polo Grill was our restaurant of choice for supper and then Cade wanted to go back to our suite to relax in the Jacuzzi, before turning in early for the night. I prayed he would not touch me because, from the way I felt, I would not have coped with that. Fortunately, he displayed no interest and the evening passed by without incident. We both fell asleep quickly, rather tuckered out by the day's excursion.

The following day, we arrived at the Roman Port of Civitavecchia, which means "old city". I had been looking forward to this part of the trip, as I had always wanted to travel to Italy.

We needed to get out early that day, as we planned to travel to Rome first and that would easily take us about ninety minutes on public transport.

Once we arrived in Rome, our first visit was to The Sistine Chapel, the official residence of the Pope within the Vatican City. It is famous for its architecture and impressive frescoes painted by famous artists like Michelangelo and Botticelli. Michelangelo took at least four years to paint the ceiling of the Chapel and includes his most renowned work, the "Last Judgment". It is said that he suffered enduring impairment to his eyes, as this masterpiece was so demanding of him physically.

Then we walked to The Vatican Museum, which also houses some amazing artworks. Cade had pre-purchased entry tickets to all the places we visited, and it enabled us to skip the lines, which would generally have been a two or three-hour wait. Since we are both artists, this was a thought-provoking and exciting part of the trip for us.

Afterwards, we went for a stroll around the beautifully manicured and formal Vatican Gardens. Cade had also reserved tickets for the guided tour, which was well worth it since we gleaned valuable information from the guide, who was very knowledgeable.

Saint Peter's Basilica was next. A late Renaissance church, whose architecture is regarded as the greatest building of its age, the complex design is the product of a number of artists, but in particular, once more, Michelangelo. During the year, the pope himself presides over several services, drawing crowds of tens of thousands.

By this time, we were rather hungry, and went to have lunch at The Dome restaurant, housed in the Starhotels Michelangelo. It seemed particularly fitting because of our admiration for the incredible artistic talent of the man, and we had a pleasant late lunch in a lovely setting.

Immediately afterwards, we had to make our way back to Civitavecchia and were sorry that we would not have much time to explore further. We had travelled all the way to Rome and not been able to see everything we would have liked. We decided right there to visit again, sometime in the future.

It was a wonderful, but particularly tiring day. We had been exploring on foot for two full days, and both felt the effects of the exercise. We decided to order in-suite dinner and have another early night. Cade appeared to have lost interest in daily sex since the last awful night, and I was relieved, as I did not know how I would handle his next approach.

Day seven heralded our arrival at Livorno, Tuscany, situated along the coast of the Ligurian Sea, one of the most important ports in Italy. We spent two days there, so we decided to stay a night ashore, and take a guided tour to the cities of Florence and Pisa, where we visited many places. Among them was "Pitti Palace" which houses interesting museums, such as a Costume Gallery and Porcelain Museum.

We then went to have lunch at the Golden View Open Bar, a sophisticated Tuscan restaurant, with a view of the

"Ponte Vecchio" and situated on the Arno River. Afterwards, we took a walk over the old bridge or "Ponte Vecchio" and did a little window shopping.

We chatted quite amicably about the incredible sights we had seen on our tours, as we strolled through the Boboli Gardens. They contain a beautiful rose garden with perfectly trimmed hedges, and all things green, including a gorgeous view over the city.

That night, we stayed at the Villa Grand Cora Hotel; ornate, rich, indulgently Italian, and not far from the Boboli Gardens, and enjoyed a gourmet dinner at the "Il Pasha" restaurant.

Next morning early, after breakfast, we headed for Pisa to see the famous "Campanile" or Leaning Tower. We took dozens of photographs, as we had of each place we had visited.

On our return to Livorno, we went to the Sanctuary of Montenero on a hill overlooking scenic Livorno. "The Shrine of Our Lady of Grace" is a Basilica, tended by Vallumbrosan monks. The sanctuary holds some lovely paintings and the sacred image of the Madonna of Montenero can be found in the Chapel of the Virgin.

Although we had eaten an early breakfast, we were feeling hungry, so before visiting any more sights, we stopped at "Ristorante La Fonte del Penitente" for a seafood lunch.

We then decided to take a boat tour along the "fossi" or canals around the "Fosso Reale" or Royal Canal, past the "Fortezza Nuova" or New Fortress and right under the "Piazza della Repubblica" previously called the "Big Bridge".

Then it was time for a late afternoon coffee, and traditional Italian pastry, Cannoli, which I enjoyed in a hazelnut flavour and Cade's was chocolate cream.

All too soon, we returned to The Nautica; filled with the sights, sounds, and smells of Livorno, Tuscany. Another day that ended with a relaxing Jacuzzi and a light supper in our suite, before collapsing into bed.

Monte Carlo was our next stop the following morning, and I was looking forward to visiting the Royal Palace, official residence of His Royal Highness Prince Albert II, who married a South African, Charlene Witstock, born in Zimbabwe, and a world-renowned medal-winning swimmer.

The Royal Palace of Monaco was built by the Genoese and overlooks the city and sea. Opulent rooms are inlaid with marble in mosaic designs, walls are draped in silk brocades and damask, and hung with royal portraits painted by famous artists.

The legendary Monte-Carlo Casino, or "The Grande Casino de Monaco", in its elegant setting was our destination for lunch at the terrace restaurant "Le Privés", with its large picture windows offering an enchanting view of the sea and Cap-Martin.

After lunch, Cade wanted to do some gambling, while I took a wander around and went to relax alongside one of the hotel swimming pools.

Not surprisingly, Cade won a significant sum of money that day, and the Casino treated us like royalty, inviting us to enjoy a free dinner at "Le Grill". We could not resist the offer and stayed to enjoy gourmet cuisine with an incredible view of the Mediterranean Sea before returning to the ship.

Next, The Nautica docked at the port of Marseilles, the capital of the Provence-Alpes-Côte d'Azur region. Although I was eager to explore the city, I was somewhat hesitant as well, having heard that the French are not friendly to English-speaking people. But here, the rumour was proven wrong, as the residents were warm and welcoming.

Château Borély was our first stop, as Cade and I were interested in seeing the three museums housed within, namely the Museum of Earthenware, that of Fashion, and of Decorative Arts. The ceiling of the entrance hall is decorated by an elaborate fresco, and from here, one enters the main reception room with a beautiful view overlooking the French gardens, which we explored after visiting the exhibitions.

Then we went on to one of the most famous and iconic churches in Marseilles, the "Basilica of Notre Dame de la Garde", built on the highest point of the city, which was next on our itinerary. An abundance of ornate gold leaf is found on the interior walls of the upper sanctuary. Also, depicted in the intricate ceiling and floor mosaics, are exotic birds, palm trees, olives, and vines, with the city's maritime connections prominently displayed in anchor motifs, life buoys, model boats, and even a ship with sails bearing the blue and white colours of Marseilles, above the altar.

Two artworks which stood out to me in the interior were a silver statue of the Virgin Mary and the Florentine "Annunciation". The views of Marseilles from the wraparound terraces are magnificent. The epic gold leaf coated statue of the Virgin dominates the top of the building.

We decided to have lunch at Notre Dame's restaurant, "L'Eau Vive", before once more descending the long staircase to catch the "petit train" back to the port.

On our return journey, we explored the "Cathédrale Sainte-Marie-Majeure de Marseille or Cathédrale de la Major", which is the main Catholic Roman Cathedral of Marseilles. The front of this imposing building has an unusual multi-coloured stone "striped" pattern which is found on the exterior and repeated within. A variety of flags from different countries are prominently on display inside.

At "Le Panier Gourmand", we enjoyed a late afternoon cup of coffee and a "mille-feuille" or custard slice which has layers of pastry alternating with crème pâtissière. Then it was time once more to board The Nautica, for the final leg of our journey.

Since this was our last night aboard the ship and it was also my twenty-first birthday, Cade had arranged for us to have supper at the intimate Polo Grill, with its timeless elegance and Hollywood legends captured in black and white photographs on the walls.

We had both dressed up in all our finery and were about to leave the suite when my husband surprised me with a small, beautifully wrapped gift box.

"Happy Twenty-First Birthday, Amber," he announced, smiling with glee.

Intrigued, I took my present and quickly opened it. Nestled inside was a gold ring adorned with an oval fire opal, my birthstone. It was striking and fitted my finger perfectly.

"Thank you, Cade. What a gorgeous gift and so unexpected on top of this wonderful cruise." I kissed him full on the lips with delight.

"It is my pleasure, lovely lady. I thought it is only fitting that you have a keepsake to remember this vacation and a significant birthday. We had better get going, before I decide to skip supper and go straight to dessert," he said with the gleam of desire in his eye.

I hastily agreed and whisked him out of the room. As good as things were at that moment, the memory of him violating me was still fresh in my mind.

Our delicious dinner consisted of perfectly cooked fillet steaks, accompanied by lightly steamed fresh vegetables, and topped off with a decadent seven-layer Belgian chocolate fudge cake.

The wait staff of the restaurant brought my slice of cake topped with a sizzling sparkler, and to my embarrassment, they proceeded to sing "Happy Birthday" to me. Nevertheless, it was the perfect ending to an equally perfect day. Even though we were rather tired, we decided to go for one last walk around the ship before returning to our suite to pack bags, in preparation for disembarkation the following day.

The next morning, we docked early in Barcelona, and Cade had planned yet another surprise. He had reserved a suite for us at the five-star Hotel Arts, Barcelona, for the day;

paid a premium for us to book in early, so we could deposit our luggage, freshen up, and do some sightseeing.

Our first stop was the "Parc de la Ciutadella", which consisted of a stunning fountain, lake, some museums, and a zoo, through which we took a leisurely stroll. Afterwards, we took a coffee break and sampled a "Spanish Palmera" - a sweet and flaky, scroll-like pastry.

Cade and I then made our way to the fascinating gothic Barcelona Cathedral with a roof featuring gargoyles and a variety of domestic and mythical creatures. The cathedral is dedicated to Saint Eulalia, whose body is also entombed in the crypt.

We walked through the "El Barri Gotic", which is the gothic quarter of Catalonia, Barcelona, and on to "Las Ramblas", a pedestrian market with dozens of outdoor cafes, where we had a light lunch, before heading back to our hotel to freshen up.

Our Mediterranean adventure had come to an end. It was time to grab our bags and head for the airport, to catch our flight home to South Africa.

Chapter 18

Life continued in its usual routine. Holidays and seasons came and went, with nothing remarkable happening. I carried on with my degree at Varsity and Cade worked hard for his next exhibition.

It was at least a month after we returned home from the cruise before we made love again. My husband was as gentle and tender as he had always been, before that dreadful night aboard The Nautica. At first, I found myself stiffening up with fearful anticipation, but gradually that wore off as the joy of lovemaking won me over once more.

In the second year of our marriage, I completed my Bachelor of Fine Arts Degree and graduated from University. With great enthusiasm, I began to work on my own art pieces for an exhibition. Like Cade, I also enjoyed painting scenery, however, unlike his preference for oils, my medium was water-colours. I had started working on a couple of sketches of Hout Bay when I remembered the one I first saw of Cade's work at the beach the day we met.

I wondered what had happened to that picture because I knew he wanted to keep it as a memento of our meeting, so I doubted he had taken it to the gallery. Wandering through our home, I searched in various places for it. I cleared out cupboards and looked in larger drawers. It was nowhere to be found in the house so it was possible that he had taken the artwork to the gallery for display.

But a thought began to niggle at the back of my mind, and I wondered if he might have stowed it in the outside room, where he kept his mother's pictures, and some of his own that did not go on display.

Cade kept the storeroom securely locked to keep the artwork safe, and I had no idea where he held the key. I looked around to see if I could find one with the bunch of spare keys in the kitchen cabinet, but it was not there. I knew he had one key that he kept himself and I suspected there was a second one in his desk drawer in the study. I had been in there many times, and the top drawer was always locked. Nevertheless, on this particular day, I was mysteriously drawn back to search that desk.

Sitting on my husband's burgundy leather chair, I turned my attention to the right side of the desk and with bated breath, I reached out my hand to tug at the top drawer. I drew in a quick breath of surprise. After the sound of a sharp click, it slid open with ease. It had not been properly locked.

Hardly believing my luck, I peered into the opening. There it was, a large brass key for a padlock, lying right on top. It had a tiny artist's pallet keyring attached to it, with a label which read, "Storeroom Key".

I picked it up gingerly, my heart beating rapidly, and gazed at it hesitantly for a couple of seconds. Gathering all my courage, I took the key and went as quickly as I could to the outside room. It was only midday, so I was quite convinced Cade would be working until late that night.

Under the shade of a large tree, at the bottom of the garden, stood a very sombre looking building. The wooden planks were dark and worn with age, bits of moss clinging here and there, but still managed to look sturdy. Paint was peeling off the black door, to reveal beneath the layers of red, green, and white.

There were only two windows I could see and one was covered. However, there was one high above the door that was very attractive. It was stained-glass, incorporating the shape of a butterfly. That beauty struck me as particularly odd. It seemed entirely out of place, set in this strangely haunted looking building.

Taking a deep breath, I stepped forward to open the padlock, and thought, 'What artistic wonders are hidden inside?' With that in mind, I slid the key into the padlock. It fit perfectly and clicked open. Removing the lock, and pulling open the latch, I pushed the door, and it swung awkwardly inwards with a groan. I stepped into the gloomy interior, it was as dark as pitch. The normal window was covered by a thick, black curtain, and very faint light shone through the stained-glass butterfly.

I switched on the ceiling light, which was a bare bulb, and the sudden harsh glare made me blink a few times until my eyes adjusted. On either side of the door were art supplies, shelves gathering cobwebs covered in old and new paint containers, with a variety of brushes. On one side was an easel, which held a canvas with a partial portrait. I moved gingerly farther into the room where hundreds of covered paintings were stacked.

I drew in another deep breath and tentatively lifted the corner of one of the cloths. A savagely wild, dark, and disturbing scene filled the canvas. I let out a sharp shriek and instinctively stepped back, pulling the fabric off the painting. A puff of dust filled the atmosphere, catching me in the lungs. I began to cough uncontrollably and stood in the open doorway gasping for air.

When the coughing subsided and I could breathe again, I took a good hard look at the exposed image. It was mostly red, black, and bright orange, with human beings falling off a cliff and into a raging fire in a dark pit. Coming out of the flames was a hideous face, laughing demonically. It looked like the way I would imagine hell. I dropped the cloth as if I had been burned by that fire and a shudder ran down my spine. My heart raced, and confused thoughts filled my mind. This was not what I thought would be here.

Feeling highly agitated, I moved as quickly as I could. After examining various canvasses filled with more alarming images, I finally located the Hout Bay scene I was searching for. I dusted off the spare easel and placed the work on it so I could study it better.

I stood back and gazed at the scene before me. It appeared different to how I remembered it, wilder, more chaotic somehow, and something about it made me feel uneasy. Both ocean and sky were darker and gloomier than I recalled, the massive rolling waves savage and threatening. Hout Bay hill seemed austere and foreboding. There was a tiny fishing vessel, which looked as it if was about to capsize. I imagined demonic faces projected in the sea and clouds about to pounce on this helpless boat. I decided to pack it away where I had uncovered it. This was not the inspiration I had been looking for. I felt very bewildered and unsettled.

Making sure everything was left just as I found it, I put the padlock back on the door and returned to the house. Making a hasty decision, I went as quickly as I could to the nearest locksmith and had a duplicate key made for myself.

Upon coming back home, I returned Cade's key to its hiding place, and slammed the drawer closed, thus making sure it locked. He would never know that I had been sneaking around in there. Nor would he suspect that I now had access to the storeroom. Heaving a sigh of relief at having accomplished this task, I went to find a secret place to stow my key.

Weeks passed before I thought about the Hout Bay image again, but one afternoon I plucked up the courage to venture out once more. I noticed instantly, upon entering the outside building, that things were different. There seemed to be fewer paintings, and items had been moved around. I was surprised because I did not even realise that Cade had been out there. The thought briefly crossed my mind that perhaps somebody had broken in and stolen the missing pieces. Then I noticed the windows were intact and the padlock on the door was apparently still the same one, as I had just unlocked it with my new key. I felt somewhat relieved, but perturbed.

I had to lift every cover-cloth in my effort to find the Hout Bay picture again. Seeing the hideous paintings once more, which Cade's mom had produced, really upset me, and search as I might, I could not find the artwork I was looking for.

I lifted the last dustcover and opened my mouth in a gasp of utter astonishment and disbelief. There was a portrait of me, based on the early sketches Cade had done when we met. I did not even know he had finished it, he never said a word to me, and I forgot to ask. Following the whirlwind of events that surrounded our wedding, the portrait had gone out of my mind.

The most shocking thing about the painting was not that Cade had completed it in secret and hidden it in the storeroom, but that the entire picture was slashed to ribbons. If not for the fact that the face was recognisable to me because it was mine, I would have had no clue as to who was in the portrait.

I stood rooted to the spot, frozen with fear.

'Why on earth would he do such a thing?' The worst scenarios came to mind. 'Cade hates me... Maybe he wants to slash me to pieces like that. He wants me dead.' I began to wonder if he was truly dangerous, with the genuine potential to kill me. Panic came over me.

I stumbled out of the shed, through the house, out the front door, and ran down the street until I could no longer breathe. My mind whirling, I leaned against a lamppost and tried to catch my breath. I sucked air into my lungs and let out a sob with each exhale. I was trembling all over. After a while, I began to calm down and tried to process what I had just seen. Slowly, I turned around and walked back up the hill to the house. I was having a mental conversation with myself, and by the time I got home, was convinced I had imagined it all.

'Perhaps I misunderstood Cade's reasons for slashing the painting. It's possible he was not happy with the final product and hacked it in frustration. Maybe the desecration of the artwork has more to do with Cade's feelings and expectations and less to do with me. That's it! He was unhappy about the way it turned out, and that's also the reason he had never shown it to me. That's also why he tried to destroy it.'

Satisfied with my explanations and rationale, I went into the storeroom, re-covered the picture, and set it back where it belonged. I checked around to make sure I left things precisely the way I had found them, returned my key to its hiding place, and sat down in the living-room to wait for him to come home. I had questions, and I needed answers.

It was many hours later, after I cooked the evening meal, and ate my supper alone that Cade arrived. It was past midnight, and I was already in bed, although, not sleeping. I lay there, contemplating the impending discussion as the minutes ticked by, gazing wide-eyed at the ceiling.

When I heard the car pull into the driveway, I quickly got up, put on my bathrobe and slippers, and went to find him. He was just entering the kitchen through the door that led to the garage when I walked in and switched on the light.

Cade looked startled. "Hey, Honey. Why are you up? I thought you would be in dreamland by now."

"I was in bed," I replied, "but could not get to sleep. I thought I'd have some warm milk and honey and see if that helps. I was on my way to the kitchen when I heard you arrive. If you like, I can warm your dinner and sit with you while you eat?"

He looked at me strangely for a second, then smiled, and said, "That would be great. I'll go wash up."

I heated his supper and made my hot drink then sat on one of the chairs at the kitchen counter waiting for him to return.

When he joined me, he set about eating like a starving man and in-between bites, enquired about my day.

"Well…" I said hesitantly, "I was busy with a water-colour of Hout Bay today, so I got to thinking about the one you did and wondered what happened to it."

"I'm not sure; I think I sold it."

'I suppose that explains why it's no longer in the shed.' I thought. "As I was pondering over that painting," I continued, "I wanted to ask if you ever finished the portrait I sat for. The one you started when we met."

He looked abruptly at me, a harsh, angry look coming over his face. "No. Why?" His eyes were dark, clouded over, but seemed to pierce right through me.

I started trembling, but said as calmly and casually as I could, "No reason. I merely thought about the Hout Bay painting, and when we met, so I was curious to know if you had ever completed my portrait."

I could see him visibly relax and almost smile. "I never finished that portrait and forgot all about it. Now that you have reminded me, I think I will get back to it. Of course, you will have to sit for me again some time."

Hoping he didn't notice my hesitation, I smiled back awkwardly, and said, "Oh, yes, I would love to."

By now, Cade was finished with supper. A familiar look of desire came over his face as he reached out his hand, took mine, and said, "It's late, Honey, let's get to bed."

Without saying another word, I placed my hand in his and followed him to the bedroom, all the while trying to fathom why he had blatantly lied.

Chapter 19

A month passed after that night, and I managed to put all the disturbing thoughts from my mind, trying to get going again with my water-colour painting. I had been feeling somewhat lacklustre and tired, also a little nauseous upon rising the past few days, so I hoped I wasn't coming down with something.

This specific morning, I had my breakfast, instantly felt awful, and promptly puked. Something was apparently wrong, and I made an appointment to see Dr Gooding.

When I described the vague symptoms I had been experiencing—I mainly felt fatigued, nauseous, and generally out of sorts, plus the morning vomiting—the doctor smiled, and I thought he was extremely rude until he asked the following question.

"Do you suppose you might be pregnant?"

I was dumbfounded. I was on the pill, but nothing is a hundred percent sure, so the possibility was there. I just had not thought of it. "I guess… could be," I blurted. "It's possible, perhaps even likely, but that had not previously occurred to me."

"Then let's do some tests and see if that is the case before we proceed with any treatments."

I gave him a urine sample, and while he was testing that, I went to see the nurse, who drew blood to send away to a laboratory. When I returned to his examination room, the doctor was grinning from ear to ear.

"I don't want to get too excited at this point, but from the urine analysis alone, it would appear that you are pregnant. However, we will need the blood test results to confirm it."

I was thrilled and anxious all at the same time. "Thank you, doctor," I said. "So… what should I do in the meantime and can you give me something for the nausea?"

He wrote out a prescription, advised me to eat well, and rest sufficiently until the pregnancy was verified.

I left his rooms almost dancing down the passage.

Although I was delighted about the possibility of having a baby, I decided not to tell Cade straight away, to rather wait, until I had the results to prove I was expecting. I did not know how he was going to react to this news, so it would also give me time to work on a plan to approach him.

The following night was Saturday, and I knew Cade was going to be home, so I planned a nice romantic dinner, with the idea to feel him out about his viewpoint concerning children and our future.

In the morning, I made my mental preparations, mulling over in my mind exactly how I was going to broach this tricky subject.

Later in the day, I set up a lovely dinner upstairs on our outside patio. We had a round glass and bronze wrought iron table, which I covered with a lace cloth. Then I laid out crystal glasses and silverware with a posy of fresh-cut flowers from the garden, and about a dozen aromatic candles ready to light. Pretty napkins were tucked into the glasses, and I set a bottle of sparkling grape juice in an ice bucket to chill. Supper was going to be served on a new dinner service I had recently bought, which were white with a splash of colourful poppies.

When Cade arrived home, a delicious dinner of roast lamb with mint sauce and gravy, accompanied by glazed carrots, steamed asparagus with Hollandaise sauce, roast potatoes, and garlic-butter mushrooms, was almost ready. He just had time to have a quick shower before we ate.

While we tucked into our shrimp cocktail hors d'oevres, Cade started the conversation.

"So, Honey, what is the special occasion that calls for such a delicious meal on a Saturday evening?" He asked when we sat down.

"Nothing in particular, my Love. I wanted to spend time with my gorgeous husband and show him how much he means to me."

Cade smiled, leaned across the table, and kissed me lovingly!

"Okay," I said pulling away. "Slow down, Casanova. Let's eat our dinner before we get to the dessert."

"Aww, Amber, please may I have my pudding now?"

I tried scowling, but he was irresistible and looked up at me pleadingly with those innocent blue eyes.

"No," I said as sternly as I could muster. "Supper first."

I stood up to serve the next course, and Cade grabbed me around the waist, drawing me down onto his lap. He began to kiss and caress me in the exact fashion I knew would lead us to the bedroom.

I pulled away, laughing and wagging my finger at him. I cleared away the dirty plates and brought back new ones laden with the roast I had prepared.

As night fell, Cade refilled our glasses with the sparkling grape juice and lit the candles. I was surprised he had not asked where the wine was. However, it was quite a relief that I did not have to explain the lack of alcohol just yet.

We savoured our delicious food, and I finally managed to muster the courage to bring up the future, with children as part of the conversation. "Tell me, Cade, we have now been married for over two years, and I was wondering, how many children do you see us having some day?"

I saw him literally stiffen and emotionally withdraw from me.

"Not that I am in a hurry. No pressure…" I babbled. "I merely wondered if you had ever thought about it and how you might imagine that scenario."

He leaned back in his chair and visibly relaxed before answering. "Amber, that's just it, we've only been married for a couple of years, and we should enjoy this time together. It would not be fair on any of us to have a family right now. I am at work a great deal of time and would prefer to have more to spend with our children."

"I understand what you're saying, and I agree that would be ideal, but life doesn't always work that way. What if I fell pregnant without planning to?"

"That's not going to happen if you are taking precautions," he responded. "You are still on the pill, aren't you?"

"Yes," I lied. "I simply wanted to talk to you about it, as we have never discussed the subject of babies before. And the reason I raised the subject tonight was so I could hear about your feelings regarding children."

I tried to appear cool, calm, and collected, but I was shaking inside. Not only had I deliberately lied to my husband—I was not on the pill, had stopped taking it when the doctor mentioned the probability of pregnancy—but was already expecting, and did not know what to do next.

The next moment, Cade stood up, pulled me towards him, and lifted me into his arms. "Let's not worry about that tonight. But how about we have a little fun practising?"

I smiled nervously and nodded, not trusting myself to speak. Then I lay my head on his shoulder and closed my eyes, surrendering myself to whatever would be.

Chapter 20

Days later, I called the doctor's office. The test results were positive; I was pregnant. Cade and I were going to have a son or daughter. I was simultaneously excited and terrified.

As the weeks passed, I was still not able to discuss my impending condition with the father of my child. I knew I had to do something because it was going to become evident soon enough and then I would have to deal with it no matter what. I could not fathom how I was going to broach the subject again with a man who obviously had no interest whatsoever in a future generation.

I was however, thankful that Cade had been extremely busy preparing for a forthcoming exhibition, which was keeping him away from home every day of the week. He left for work before the sun came up, so he never witnessed me being ill with morning sickness. He regularly returned late at night, long after I had gone to sleep. He was apparently also exhausted, because he did not bother me at all and that was a huge relief.

There was no one I could discuss the situation with. I had eventually lost contact with my varsity friends, who had moved on with their lives and transferred to other parts of the country.

Sadly, and for a multitude of reasons, I could not talk to my sister either. Firstly, she was not even aware that Cade and I were married, as I had not invited her to the wedding, or had any contact with her in two years. There was so much explaining to do; I did not know where to begin.

Secondly, I knew that if I called Crystal and she forgave me for not telling her before, she would hop on a plane straight away to be with me. Her unannounced visit would not fly with Cade, and then I would have to tell him the truth in any case.

I thought about going to see Cade's mother, although I had never met her. She had dementia, so even if she had been introduced to me, or if Cade had told her something about me, it was very likely that she would not know who I was, and in her state, what possible help or support could she offer?

More time went by, and I was already more than three months along. There was a small, barely perceptible bump forming in my belly, and it was only a matter of time before Cade noticed that I was swelling, and putting on weight.

Finally, one night, a few weeks later, I made up my mind to come right out and tell him. I had been psychologically preparing myself for days and devised the way I was going to reveal it.

As he was still working long days and well into the nights, I knew it was pointless to arrange a meal together or an outing, because he only came home in the early hours of the morning. Instead, I decided to wait up for him and blurt it all out.

Everything was planned meticulously. I made a delicious lamb stew accompanied by a delightful merlot wine, which was one of Cade's favourites. Then I left a note on the chocolate mousse and placed it in the fridge, alongside the plate of stew. It read, "All my love, forever, Amber xxx."

I was not going to join him while he ate his meal. The plan was to wait until he finished his supper and came to bed. Hopefully, he would be relaxed and receptive after a tasty dinner with a good glass of wine.

It was a struggle to stay awake; the pregnancy made me so tired that I was usually asleep quite early. I had taken a nap in the afternoon and eaten an early supper, then prepared myself for the evening ahead. After my bath, I chose to wear a pretty negligee with a matching robe and settled down in one of the comfy chairs in our bedroom to read.

When I heard the car driving up the road, I quickly turned off the bedroom light and sat quietly in the dark, waiting for him to come inside. My heart was going pitter-patter inside my chest.

I knew his routine well, and it was always the same. He would pull the car into the garage and enter the kitchen through the adjoining door. Anything he was carrying would be placed on the nearest counter, he would go to the fridge and remove his plate of food, which he then popped into the microwave. While his dinner was heating, he would pour himself a beverage, sometimes a glass of wine, and go through the mail I had left stacked for him.

Once his food was ready, he would sit at the kitchen table and glance through the day's newspaper while he ate. Then, he rinsed the dirty dishes and placed them in the dishwasher. Afterwards, he would make his way to the bedroom and take a quick shower before coming to bed. Sometimes waking me up, if he was in the mood for sex and wasn't too tired.

This night was no different to any other, except that he seemed to be taking longer than usual to finish in the kitchen. I smiled to myself in the dark, thinking that he was probably enjoying the chocolate mousse. The thought made me feel all warm inside, and I wanted to be with him. Then I recalled why I was awake and what I needed to divulge. I began to feel anxious again, my heart racing, and closed my eyes, taking deep breaths to calm myself down.

Eventually, I heard him switch off the kitchen light and head towards the bedroom. I quickly hopped into the bed, so that it looked as if I had been sleeping and sat up as he put on his bedside light.

"Hi, Honey, what are you doing up? Did I disturb you?"

"No, Darling, I was waiting for you."

A grin spread across his face. "That's very sweet, Amber, but I am utterly exhausted, and all I want is to sleep right now."

"That's okay," I began. "Because I just wanted to tell you something. I have news, and I did not want to wait one more minute."

Cade sat down on the bed and took my hand in his. "Now what can be so important that it cannot wait until morning and you have to tell me tonight?"

My heart began to thump furiously in my chest, and my palms became sweaty. I was so nervous I could hardly speak. "I… I need… to tell you…"

"Go on, Honey, spit it out. I don't have all night."

"Cade… my love, you know that I would never do anything on purpose to upset you?"

He pulled his hand away and stood up, a sombre look coming over his face. His voice was low and harsh. "Amber, just tell me what is going on!"

My voice choked in my throat and I barely managed to whisper. "I'm pregnant."

The words hung in the air like wisps of smoke.

Cade stood in astonished silence for a moment then turned and began to walk out of the room.

I climbed out of bed, calling after my husband. "Where are you going? Can't we talk about this?"

"Just leave it, Amber, we can talk about it in the morning! I'm going to sleep upstairs in the spare bedroom." He stormed out.

Foolishly, I followed him, tears streaming down my face. "But, Cade, this is our baby, yours and mine. I want you to be happy with me."

Without saying a word, he continued marching up the stairs.

I ran up behind him, and as he reached the top of the stairs, I grabbed his arm beseechingly.

"LEAVE ME ALONE!" he shouted, pushing me away from him.

I lost my balance and began to fall down the stairs. It happened so quickly I did not even have time to grab the banister and tumbled backwards, rolling over and over, until I landed on the floor. I lay unconscious in the entrance hall, blood oozing onto the tiles, and pooling around my limp body.

Chapter 21

"Amber! Amber, please wake up. It was an accident; I didn't mean to push you. Please forgive me. Don't leave me!" Cade sobbed and lightly stroked my head with a shaking hand.

I heard the voice calling me, echoing peculiarly in my head, as if way off in the distance. My mind was foggy, and my eyes were so heavy, it felt as if they were glued together. I desperately tried to force my mouth to open, so that I could answer him, but it remained tightly closed.

'Where am I?' It was as if I were dreaming, but the touch of his hand was quite real. I tried to make my eyelids open but they would not obey. 'Why can't I wake up? What happened to me?' I could feel my eyelashes fluttering tremulously, as my eyelids strained to pull apart from each other. Nevertheless, my eyes remained shut.

Cade must have seen the slight movement, because the next second, he was shouting. "Doctor! Doctor! Her eyelids moved, Amber must be trying to open her eyes."

Then I heard a voice that I did not recognise.

"Take it easy, Mr Raine. Your wife is in a coma, so she may be able to hear you. However, it could still be a while before she comes out of it. Mrs Raine's body sustained severe trauma from the fall, and the shock to her system after losing so much blood, and the emergency caesarean, cannot be underestimated. It has only been seven days since you brought her in. It could still take several more days, weeks, possibly even months, for her to fully come back to us."

I could hear the sobs catching in Cade's throat as he replied. "Do you think it is helpful for me to be here, holding her hand, talking to her?"

"Yes, I do," said the doctor. "There are many accounts of patients in comas being able to hear their loved ones, even if they are unable to respond. Some even claim that is what they clung to while unconscious and it gave them hope. There is also reason to believe that the physical contact will speed up recovery."

It did take several more weeks before I came out of the coma completely. During that time, I still felt as if I was living in a dream, which turned into a nightmare. Because the stronger I became, the more I remembered about what had taken place, and I did not want to wake up and face the truth.

Cade pushed me down the stairs.

He may not have meant to harm me, but neither did he consider what he was doing when lashing out at me at the top of the staircase. I believe he was consumed with rage and unthinkingly shoved me so hard, I tumbled down.

So, here I was, trapped in my own body, afraid to wake up, face my husband, and deal with the loss of our baby. I shuddered to think what the future might hold.

In my heart, I admitted to my own stupidity. I should have never chased Cade up those stairs when he was so angry. But that was what puzzled me the most. 'Why was his anger so extreme?'

A flash of memory came to my mind as I lay there contemplating that fateful day, and it was a smell. As Cade turned to push me away, the overwhelming stench of alcohol dominated his breath. I assumed he only had a single glass of wine with supper, but he was not acting like himself. In retrospect, I considered the fact that he must have imbibed the entire bottle, as I recalled him taking longer than usual to finish in the kitchen. I couldn't know anything for sure, or even if it would have made a difference. But I did know he had no wish for a baby, and he would have been furious either way, with or without the influence of alcohol. The only thing I was sure of now, was that I wanted answers when I woke up.

One morning, weeks later, I surfaced from the coma. I must have been sleeping and having a pleasant dream because I opened my eyes and momentarily felt happy. Until I saw that I was still in the hospital, hooked up to all kinds of machines and the reality of what had occurred hit me. I began to cry quietly then tried to move. I felt sore all over, my body seemed heavy and uncomfortable.

Just at that moment, a nurse came rushing in. Evidently, the noises the machines made were an alarm to alert the staff. "Mrs Raine, you are awake! How do you feel? My name is Florence."

"Flo-rence…" I croaked. Realising my throat was parched, I pointed to it with one finger.

Florence brought over a glass of water and held it to my lips.

I took a long swig and almost choked. Then, feeling a bit better, I began to speak again, my voice barely a whisper. "What happened to me? Why am I in the hospital?"

"You had a serious fall, Mrs Raine. The doctor will be here shortly, and he will explain everything."

"Where… is my husband?"

"It's a little early for visiting hours, Ma'am. But he is usually here by six or seven and stays well into the evening. Mr Raine has even spent a couple of nights in a spare bed, especially during the first week, when he was so worried about you after the accident."

I muttered under my breath, "It was no accident."

"Excuse me; I didn't catch that. What did you say?"

"Nothing, absolutely nothing," I said. My hand was shaking badly as I tugged at the sheet constricting my body. "I just need to know what is going on and when the doctor will see me."

"He'll be here soon," Florence reiterated patiently. Naturally, she had only so much authority to impart information. "In the meantime," she continued with a smile, "can I bring you tea or coffee and breakfast?"

"Yes, please. What am I allowed to have?"

"Something light. A little scrambled egg with toast? Would you like that?"

"It sounds wonderful; I feel ravenous."

"You may not be able to eat as much as you think," Florence pointed out. "You have been on intravenous fluids for a long time, but it will be good if you can get something down."

"Thank you, Florence. Could I get a small glass of orange juice as well as the coffee?"

"Certainly, Ma'am, I will order your breakfast and bring it to you shortly."

"Please call me Amber. May I get up to go to the bathroom first?"

"Not right now," said Florence quickly. "The doctor inserted a catheter while you were unconscious and it must be removed before you can go by yourself. Sister Theresa will take care of that after lunch. Try to relax, you have just come out of a six-month-long coma, so you have to take it easy until you get your strength back."

"Okay," I said and laid my head back on the pillows. I was tired already and had only been awake and talking for a few minutes.

I must have dozed off because it was the tantalising smell of coffee that roused me a short while later. I was a bit disoriented, but the information Florence had given me was starting to come back.

She cranked up the top half of the bed until I was in a sitting position, and pulled the movable table in front of me. I tucked into what tasted like the most delicious food on earth. I hadn't eaten for many weeks and was famished. Even though they had me on a glucose drip, it is not the same as eating real food and I had lost a lot of weight.

As Florence predicted, I could not stomach much, merely taking a few bites, although savouring every mouthful. Subsequently, I settled down to wait for Cade to arrive. There were a lot of questions to be asked, and hopefully answered.

The next thing I knew, Nurse Florence was waking me again, first to tell me that Cade had not been to visit yet, and that it was time for lunch already.

On the food tray was chicken soup and a bread roll. Although I had not eaten much, I still felt full from breakfast. The soup was tasty and strangely comforting.

After lunch, Sister Theresa came to remove the catheter and brought a wheelchair to get me to the bathroom.

"Am I going to be so weak that I can't walk to the toilet?" I asked.

"Yes, you probably are," replied Sister Theresa, "But it's more than that. You received a traumatic blow to your spine falling down the stairs, and you are paralysed from the waist down."

I drew in a shocked breath and covered my mouth with my hand, tears welling up in my eyes. I felt as if I were going to faint. "I'm paralysed? No, I can't be!"

"Don't panic, Mrs Raine, the doctor believes it's only temporary. It may take a while before you can walk again, even so, he is confident that you will. Try not to fret about it, just concentrate on building up your strength, and it will work out in time."

Sister Theresa carefully removed the catheter then called Nurse Florence to take me to the bathroom, where I brushed my teeth, washed my face, and completed my general ablutions as best I could under the circumstances. It took a great deal of effort, and I was exhausted when done.

Just as Nurse Florence wheeled me back into the room, Cade arrived, and when I saw him an involuntary shiver of fear ran down my spine.

He had a concerned look on his face, which was thin and gaunt, as if he too had lost weight. In his hands was a beautiful bouquet of Strelitzias and Frangipanis, which he placed gently on my lap. Then he knelt in front of the wheelchair and took my hands into his.

I stiffened with anger and alarm.

"Oh, Amber, my Love, you are awake. I so wanted to be here when you regained consciousness, and I cannot tell you how pleased I am that you are out of the coma. I have been so worried about you all these months. How are you feeling?"

"About as well as could be expected, Cade. The pain is not too bad, but being paralysed from the waist down is frightening, even if it may only be temporary."

"Yes, yes, the doctor told me about it. He said he is very optimistic that you will walk again. In time, you will be as good as new."

"No, Cade," I said, my voice rising. "Even if I fully recover from this, I will never be the same again. You shoved me down the stairs, and I lost our baby." I shouted and cried, waves of heart-rending sobs tearing out of my mouth and tears streaming down my face. "I don't even know if we had a daughter or a son. You killed our child! Murdered our baby!" Utterly incensed I grabbed hold of the bouquet of flowers he had brought me and hurled them across the room.

Tears welled in Cade's eyes as he looked at me. "It was an accident; I didn't mean to hurt you. I was just pushing you off me and didn't realise how close you were to the stairs. I was not thinking clearly."

"Because you were drunk. Did you finish that whole bottle of wine I left with your supper?"

"Yes, I did," he responded, "but I was not drunk. I was fully aware of what I was doing; I simply misjudged the distance to the steps. My actions had nothing to do with alcohol. I was furious because you were pregnant, when we had agreed to wait, and I could think of nothing else."

"So, it was all my fault that I was pregnant because that's how it works, is it?"

"No, of course not. You were supposed to be on the pill, and clearly, you lied to me, because you could not have been if you fell pregnant."

"Well, for your information, Mr Know-it-all, you can fall pregnant on the pill under certain conditions. I was taking antibiotics for a bladder infection around the time I fell pregnant, and it never occurred to me the pill had become obsolete. I only discovered it myself when I saw the doctor and heard I was expecting. He explained how I must have conceived while still taking contraceptives."

"Truly, Amber? I'm sorry. I didn't know that. I honestly thought you stopped taking the pill deliberately to fall pregnant and then tried to deceive me. I am genuinely regretful I did not trust you and got so angry about something you had no control over. Please forgive me. Do you think we can get past this?"

"I don't know, Cade. I am hurt, and so much more than just physically. I have to constantly walk on eggshells around you and often, I am petrified of your reaction if I say the wrong thing."

"Please give me one more chance, Amber. I promise I will make it up to you, and this will never happen again."

"You're right about one thing, this will never happen again! How many chances do you think I should give you? And drinking too much is always your excuse! This is not the first time you have injured me."

"I remember your wrist, Amber. You don't have to remind me. I wasn't drunk that night."

"No, but you were on other occasions, such as our wedding night and on the cruise."

"I said I was sorry."

"I know you did. I accepted your apologies, but I have never forgotten. Forgiving you this time is going to be really hard." We sat in awkward silence for a few minutes then I asked stiffly, "Tell me, Cade, what did we have, a son or a daughter?"

In a very soft voice Cade spoke, "A little girl, our first child would have been a daughter."

Fresh tears rolled down my cheeks, and I began to sob uncontrollably. Cade placed his arms around me and tried to comfort me.

I pushed him away, still profoundly hurt and ferociously angry, and in a breathless whisper I said, "Get out of my sight, out of my room. I hate you!"

Just then the doctor walked past Cade and introduced himself to me. "Good Day, Mrs Raine, it is good to see you awake. My name is Dr James, and I have been your attending physician. How are you feeling? I can see you are upset."

Between sobs, I managed to say, "Pleased to meet you, Dr James. My husband just told me that we lost our little girl."

"I am sorry you had to be informed of such bad news so soon after coming out of the coma, and sadly, I have something else that I must tell you." Dr James hesitated, obviously trying to find the right words to say. "Mrs Raine, there is no easy way to say this, but when we delivered the foetus by caesarean section, I discovered that your uterus had ruptured and was beyond repair. Lamentably, we had to do a complete hysterectomy, and therefore, I regret that you will not be able to have children naturally."

I completely broke down at that point and began to wail and sob with anguish; for myself, my dead child, and the dreadful future that had just been presented to me. I had lost my baby, was paralysed, and would never be pregnant again. The emotional anguish was so devastating I wanted to die there and then, and wished with all my heart that I had never come out of the coma. I became quite hysterical, screaming at Cade to leave and never return.

Doctor James quickly called for a sedative and after a short time I fell into a deep sleep once more. A group of considerably troubled faces staring down at me.

Chapter 22

Days turned into weeks, weeks into months, and I was still no better. I was not able to walk, and I was confined to a wheelchair during my waking hours. Deep depression set in and I completely lost the will to live. I was a young woman in my twenties, and I wanted to die. I was still enraged and in great anguish, if not more than before, nevertheless, I kept all my emotions bottled inside.

From the first day I regained consciousness, Cade was contrite and extremely concerned about my well-being. He became the epitome of a loving, caring husband. Apologies and declarations of love poured from his lips continually, but none touched me. My heart was like ice, and I had thrown up a wall so high, I doubted it would ever come down.

After months of rehabilitation and psychotherapy, I was eventually allowed to go home. As much as I wanted to be out, I was also reluctant to leave the sanctuary of the hospital. I loathed the idea of going back to a life with Cade, the man who had killed our daughter and robbed me of the privilege of ever being able to carry another child in my womb again. But without the necessary resources to take care of myself, I had no choice. My limitations forced me to return to the place of my torment.

Everything was arranged to facilitate my life when I returned.

Cade engaged the services of a live-in nurse and hired a daily maid who could also cook and clean to take care of me. He moved into the upper-floor guestroom, so that I could remain in our master bedroom. This worked well because the nurse could use the second bedroom downstairs. He spared no expense to make sure I was comfortable and received the best of care. Even so, it meant absolutely nothing to me.

He had a motor installed on the staircase banister, so I could go upstairs in my wheelchair to get to the upper floor. However, I had no interest in going up there for any reason, not to see the sunset, the ocean from the veranda, or him! The mere thought of the upper landing or passing the stairs reminded me of that dreadful night and sent me into fits of crying.

The nurse, whose name was Valerie, tried everything she could think of to lift my spirits. She made me get up in the morning when all I wanted to do was sleep forever. Val made sure I ate well and did my exercises to keep the muscles in my legs healthy. But when I was awake, all I wanted to do was sit in my chair and mourn the loss of my baby.

If I could have managed it, I would have killed myself or left, because there seemed to be no future for me. Even if I were to walk again, I could not imagine continuing to live with the man who had murdered my child. Not only was I still paralysed physically—because, let's be realistic, so was my mind—but there was no way I could support myself. It was then I was struck with the realisation that I had no income. There was nothing I could call my own, besides my car and the few gifts Cade had given me thus far. I had never worked and while he took care of all our expenses, I occasionally used portions of my dwindling inheritance for my own needs. There was nowhere near enough money left to take care of me now that I was disabled. I had no choice but to stay.

One miserable day blurred into the next. The daily routine of just being alive was all I could handle. Getting me ready in the mornings took hours. Then there were periods of exercise, interspersed with routine visits to the hospital for physical therapy and to see the psychologist. Throughout it all, Valerie was my constant companion.

She was a compassionate, Christian woman, whose kindness to me knew no bounds. Val was not overly chatty, but we had enough conversation to make life bearable. In time, I learned a lot about this nurse who was totally dedicated to my well-being and recovery.

Sadly, she was divorced from her alcoholic husband, with whom she had spent many years raising four sons, who all had grown up and left home to make their living overseas. Val was so proud of them and visited when time and finances allowed. She had worked as a nurse all her life and had very little in the way of monetary resources. Her situation pricked my consciousness with the realisation that I had everything money could buy.

Valerie, however, had some precious things that money could not buy. Her children and grandchildren, a vocation as a nurse earning an honest living, and making a real difference in other people's lives. I cared for her dearly, but in some ways envied the simplicity of her life, and especially the love she shared with her family. These thoughts made me feel all the more useless and pathetic.

Cade and I hardly spoke to each other and he was rarely home, spending a lot of time at work. He had even taken to sleeping there most nights. I was not sure if he had set himself up in a room at the gallery or an apartment nearby, and quite honestly, I did not care. The less I saw of him, the better.

When he was around, he acted as if he was the doting, loving husband. He did not fool me—although I often wondered if he had duped Val—because in my heart, I knew it was a lie. 'How could he do this to me? To us? Did he even care that we lost our child, or that we will never have babies of our own?'

Even though I never confronted Cade again about the baby that died at his hand, inwardly I seethed with resentment. It was only through Valerie's support and encouragement that I began to come to terms with all that had happened to me.

Months went by, and Val encouraged me to try walking. The doctor's tests indicated that the paralysis had indeed been only temporary and the lower half of my body was fully functional once more, but for some reason, I still felt absurdly weak, despite the daily exercises. Now, I had to learn to walk again. I just did not have the physical or emotional energy to cope with it all.

Secretly, I admitted; if I learned to walk and recovered to a semblance of normal, I would also be forced to make decisions about my life and future, with or without Cade. I also feared Valerie leaving, because I would be alone with my abusive husband. She gave me a sense of peace and protection. Her presence was the only reason I still clung to this life.

One day, Cade came home with an idea, which he thought would perhaps motivate and inspire me to do something positive. He was going to build an extension over the garage, with an inter-leading door to the upstairs sitting room. This room was going to be my new art studio.

Strangely, for the first time in ages, I did feel a spark of energy inside, and actually became excited about the concept.

He also suggested that while the new studio was under construction, I could look at re-decorating the interior of our home. Even though Cade was a talented, well-known artist, he had sorely neglected the house. The furnishings and décor were old and drab. Everything was from his parents' time and had merely been given to him. Nothing in our home spoke of our life together.

Before I could offer excuses or forget the suggestion, Cade brought me all kinds of brochures; from paint to carpet and curtain samples, together with catalogues of every type of furniture and fitting imaginable.

I began spending my days poring over colours, fabrics, and pictures until my head swam dizzily with ideas. I also started looking forward to Cade coming home, so I could tell him all my plans. Whatever I proposed, he supported enthusiastically and said I could have whatever I desired, money was never an object.

By the time the space over the garage was completed, I had redone the interior, from front to back and top to bottom. The drab grey walls were gone, replaced with a soft cream, which was a much better match for the marble tiles and showed off all the beautiful cherry-wood furniture and fixtures.

The staircase banister, with its wrought iron leaves, was now a warm bronze, instead of stark black and the chandelier had been replaced with strings of large, amber, bubble lights, of varying lengths. The walls were filled with artworks, some from well-known artists, mine, and of course a few of Cade's commercial pieces.

I began to experience a joy and contentment that had been missing for a long time. I started looking forward to the day when I could go upstairs to my new art studio to draw and paint. Despite choosing the new look for the upstairs area and deciding on the décor for the studio, I had not yet used the banister motor to go and see for myself.

Cade was delighted with our home and plainly wanted to spend more time there, with me, and I could feel that my heart was beginning to soften towards him again. As the memory of that dreadful night slowly faded, becoming less consuming, I felt a renewed interest in life.

I woke up on the morning of the one-year anniversary since I had fallen down the stairs and lost not only our baby girl but an integral part of my womanhood, feeling deeply distressed. It seemed as if one day I moved forward and the next I was back in the throes of depression.

Val, who was not merely my nurse by this time, but also a dear friend and companion, noticed the change in my mood instantly and tackled the problem head-on. She encouraged me to talk about the experience, to cry on her shoulder, and sat quietly with me as I grieved yet again for my loss.

Then gently, she took both my hands, fixed her gaze on mine, and said, "Now, you are done! No more pity parties. No more living in the past. From this day forward, you will live in the present. You may look back and remember what happened on that fateful night, although you are no longer going to let that situation define you. I have seen such an improvement over these last few months, please don't throw it all away."

I realised at that moment that I had begun to live again, even if only partially, now, I needed to fully engage once more. Hesitantly, I spoke, "Valerie, thank you for being here and taking such good care of me. I am blessed to have you. Please help me. I want to reclaim my life and walk up those stairs on my own two feet to see my new art studio."

She smiled from ear to ear and said, "Now that is an answer to a prayer. It will be a great pleasure to help you get upstairs. We will start preparing today. Let's not say anything to your husband just yet, and show him when you're ready."

We made our clandestine pact. From that day, Val aided me tirelessly to exercise my almost atrophied legs. It was hard, much harder than I imagined, nonetheless, I was determined to succeed. Day after day, I worked at re-learning to walk, until I felt strong and a semblance of normal.

The day came when we were ready to tell Cade. I wanted to surprise him. On this occasion, I got myself up the stairs in my wheel chair, using the staircase banister motor. Then I sat in the living room, and waited for him to come home.

When he arrived, Valerie met him at the door and requested a private meeting upstairs to discuss my progress. Naturally, he agreed instantly, and they walked up together. I stood myself up as I heard their footfall on the stairs.

When they reached the landing, Val hung back for a moment, allowing Cade to enter the sitting room first. His eyes caught mine across the room and a look of disbelief flitted across his face, then he smiled broadly as he saw me standing there on my own.

I walked across the floor as quickly as I could and flung myself into his arms.

He picked me up and swung me around in delight. Then the words tumbled out of him. "What happened? When did you start walking again? Why didn't you tell me?"

"Because I wanted to surprise you," was my response. "I needed to see my new art studio for the first time with you walking beside me, not pushing my wheelchair."

Grinning happily, Cade took my hand and led me into a gorgeous studio. Evening light flooded in through the wall of ceiling-to-floor windows and lit up the room filled with the furniture I had chosen, as well as all the art supplies I could ever want.

As we stood hand in hand, taking in the stunning view of the sunset over the ocean, I began to feel hope again, not just for life, but also for our marriage, and a future with my husband for a second time.

Chapter 23

Life became the new normal, as I called it, because nothing was the same, nor would it ever be. Little by little I forgave Cade, although, I never forgot.

Nurse Valerie left once I was fully able to take care of myself. We stayed friends, and she never failed to call me on the anniversary of our daughter's death, to make sure I was okay.

Experts say time heals all wounds. Well, I'm not sure that I ever fully mended, but I was able to move forward and once more enjoy life, without being emotionally or physically debilitated. I threw myself the occasional pity party, but a call to Val always lifted my spirits and helped me cope.

I devoted much of my time to painting, and it brought me a great deal of comfort and personal satisfaction. I also began to experiment with different mediums. I still favoured water-colours, but I enjoyed the challenge of mastering new things, and the oils, gouache, and pastels produced entirely different effects.

Now and then, Cade went up to the studio to see what I had created. He was impressed with my work, especially the water-colours scenes. One day, he told me he was going to hang some of my paintings in the art gallery and have an exhibition.

I was delighted and set my mind on finishing some pieces I had started years previously, one of them being my

Hout Bay water-colour. It was not in my upstairs studio and I vaguely remembered Cade proposing storing it in the outside room while we re-decorated the house.

I was reluctant to go out to the storeroom again, but I wanted to find that painting to include in the exhibition. I found the copy of the key I had secretly made and ventured outside with trepidation.

Once inside the storeroom, I switched on the light and looked around. Things looked different yet again, notwithstanding that a year had past, and I knew Cade was spending time in there without wanting me to know about it.

I could not tell where my painting was, so once more the search entailed checking under all the dust cloths to find it. I braced myself for viewing the hideous pictures I knew were there and began to look for the one I wanted.

As I worked my way through the rows, I felt compelled to remove the artwork that had upset me before and placed the picture of Hell on the easel by the window, so that I could examine it more closely. The colours were vivid and bold, but the demonic faces even more frightening than I recalled. I shivered with disgust as I scrutinised this macabre rendition.

Better able to see the painting in the light, something in the bottom right-hand corner caught my attention. It was a signature, and one that I recognised instantly, "Cade Raine". Shocked, I looked more closely, unable to believe what I was seeing. There it was, Cade's signature, not his mother's.

'What does this mean?' It was frightening and unnerving and destroyed many assumptions I had formerly held.

Feeling a bit frantic, I moved through the rows of covered paintings, rapidly lifting the dustcovers, and checking the signatures in the bottom right-hand corner. Each and every one was signed "Cade Raine".

Had Cade painted these, or had he covered his mother's signature and then scribbled his own, making these works fraudulent? If so, to what end? Because there was no way, he was ever going to sell these hideous things. On the other hand, if these were his, then why had he lied and said his mother had painted them?

I had no idea how I was going to get to the truth, even though I realised it was essential to do so and not delay any further. But—and mainly from the jumbled theories that were now becoming overwhelming—I knew I had to broach the subject cautiously, as I did not want to rile Cade and give him any hint that I had discovered his secret. I was also fearful of incurring his wrath and perhaps unwittingly inviting a physical assault.

A few days later, I had an opportunity to speak to him and approached the topic of paintings by asking him if he could remember where he had stored my Hout Bay piece.

"Yes," he replied, "I put it in the storeroom, I'll get it for you over the weekend."

"That would be great, I appreciate it. Cade… I was wondering, is there any chance I could perhaps view your mother's artworks? They might give me some greatly needed inspiration."

His body stiffened, and a hardness came over his demeanour. "No," he said harshly. "That is out of the question. My mother's paintings are horrendous and the product of a sick mind. I do not want you to see them. Ever! Understood?"

I instantly agreed and tried to assuage his ire. "No problem, Honey, I was just curious. You know that I'm working on my pieces for the exhibition and at times I lack vision." Then quickly changing the subject, I continued. "Do you think we could go away for a weekend together and recharge, maybe for our wedding anniversary?"

He started to relax and even smiled faintly. "That sounds like a good idea. Anywhere in particular you would like to go?"

"I was thinking about the Drakensberg. There's a beautiful hotel there, called Champagne Castle and I believe the Azaleas are something to see in the springtime. I read that the walks are great, the food excellent, and the scenery breath-taking."

"Mmmm. Flowers, walks, fresh air, and mountain views… Sounds like paradise to me," he responded. "I'll consider it, and see if I can book for early October."

Relieved, I smiled, and gave him a big hug. "That would be wonderful! I can hardly wait."

Inwardly, my mind was whirling, Cade had once more lied right to my face. I needed answers, and I did not know how to get them. I did have one idea but it was a long-shot. However, I had nothing to lose at this point and made up my mind right there and then, I was finally going to meet Cade's mother.

Chapter 24

I thought this was going to take some detective work. Instead it turned out to be a simple mission. I went on the internet to search for Alzheimer care facilities in Constantia and found La Grande Auberge. I called to inquire about a patient named Mrs Elizabeth Raine, and the receptionist was quite helpful, confirming that Liza was indeed a resident there. At once I made a note of the address and planned my visit for a day when I knew for sure Cade would be tied up in meetings at the Art Gallery.

I drove out early to Constantia Village, stopping in at The Robins Coffee Shop. I spent some time there mulling over how I was going to handle this unannounced and unprepared meeting with Cade's mother. I did not want to upset her, but if possible, I hoped Liza would be able to give me some of the answers I was desperately seeking.

At about ten o'clock, I entered the gates to the complex Liza Raine called home. It was a beautiful facility set in lush gardens with stunning views. The residences were all well-appointed, with meticulous attention to detail, and the patients receive around-the-clock care.

I went straight to the reception desk to introduce myself and complete the attendance register. Sarah, the receptionist, was pleasant and noticeably glad to meet Elizabeth Raine's daughter-in-law. She was in fact, astonished that Cade and I had been married for so long and I had never visited Liza.

I explained a little about my fall, coma, and subsequent confinement to a wheelchair, although I did not elaborate too much. Sarah was very understanding and called one of the nurses to accompany me to Liza's room. They had not told her I was coming, as I planned it to be a surprise.

And it was, for both of us! More of a shock really, because within minutes of meeting this strange woman, I knew without a doubt, that not only did she not have Alzheimer's, but she was fully cognizant, and as smart as a whip.

Nurse Daily introduced me to Liza as Cade's wife, and although she did not overtly react, I could see the amazement in her eyes. She merely smiled in acknowledgement, and we were left alone. The instant the nurse left us, she called me over to sit beside her, and we started a conversation that lasted for hours.

"I am very pleased to meet you, Mrs Raine," I said formally. "My name is Amber, and I am married to your son, Cade. I'm not sure if he has ever mentioned me…"

"Please, call me Liza," she told me with a smile. "No, Cade never mentioned you. But that is no surprise, as I haven't seen my son in fifteen years, not since the day he brought me here."

The response stunned me. "I did not know that, as Cade often tells me that he comes to see you. He never allowed me to accompany him, so I have no idea where he goes when he's supposedly visiting you. His main reason is that you are too fragile and would not cope with the stress of meeting me."

"That is also not unusual. Cade would not want us to meet because then, you would find out that everything he has ever told you has been a lie."

"What do you mean?"

"Well, to start with, I'm guessing he told you that I have Alzheimer's? Because that is how he got me into this facility in the first place. He lied to the staff and forced me to co-operate. If I didn't do as he demanded, I would have been out on the street and penniless."

"Yes. Cade said you have Dementia, that you barely remember him. Also, you would not be able to cope with meeting his new wife. Why on earth would he do that, to you, to me?"

"These revelations may come as a shock to you, Amber, nevertheless, I believe you should know the truth. Cade is a sociopath, who suffers from Bipolar disorder, exacerbated by the abuse he suffered at the hands of his father when he was a young boy. He blames me for everything that happened in his life, and I bear the guilt of believing it is partly my fault because I did allow it to happen right under my nose. I tried to get him help after his father died… By then the damage was already done and deeply rooted. He hated… hates me."

Astonished yet again, I covered my mouth with both hands. "Oh, my word," I said. "That explains so much!"

"Is Cade still drinking?" asked Liza.

"Occasionally. When he does, things get out of control, very quickly. He is a different person when he drinks too much."

"His medication does not mix too well with alcohol," replied his mother.

"I did not even know he was taking anything. Not sure why he's hiding that from me. One thing I don't understand is why he insisted that you come to live here."

"For the oldest reason in the world, Amber, greed. He wanted me out of the way, so that he could have control of my money. Told me outright that if I signed my fortune over to him and agreed to live here, he would take care of me for life, on the condition he would never see me again. I was afraid of what he might do if I disagreed, so I went along with his scheme. Thankfully, I do have a good life here, and I want for nothing. Nonetheless, I do feel like such a sham, pretending to have Alzheimer's, when there are people here who genuinely have Dementia and need the care. I try to be as little trouble as possible, so as not to take the attention away from anyone else."

"Liza, something else I need to know. Tell me about the macabre paintings in our storeroom. I mean... I'm assuming you're aware of them."

Liza nodded.

"They are hideous, and Cade said that you painted them."

"No, Amber, I didn't. Cade's father was the artist, not me. It was his hobby, and I burned all the paintings after he died. They were dreadful. What do the paintings you are talking about look like?"

"One of them looks like a depiction of hell, with bright oranges, reds, and ugly dancing demons. There is even a face that looks like the devil coming out of the flames."

"That sounds like a recurring theme from many of Cade's artworks over the years. He started drawing pictures of infernos as a young boy. I tried to talk to him about it, but he would just get angry and clam up. Perhaps I should have tried harder. I did not know what to do and quite frankly, had no idea the problem was as bad as it seems to have turned out to be."

"When I met him, he was becoming well-known for his wild and evocative landscapes. He never exhibited any of the frightening paintings that are hidden away. Once, when I somehow managed to discuss art, he told me you painted some awful things. I believed him until recently, when I discovered his signature on all of them. It confused me. Why the lies, pretence, cover-up? I did not understand, and I needed answers. That is when I decided to take the chance to come see you."

"I'm glad you did, Amber. Tell me about your life, married to my son."

I told her everything, leaving nothing out, and by the end of the day, she was in tears and sobbing, as if her heart would break.

Not only did she meet the daughter-in-law she never knew she had, but she also discovered that her only granddaughter had died at her own son's hand, and that she would probably never have any more. Although she did not say it, I got the feeling she was somewhat relieved that Cade's legacy would not continue into future generations. In any event, I also knew she was heartbroken for me and what I had suffered because of him.

"What are you going to do now?" Liza asked.

"I honestly don't know what to do. After all that has happened over the years, I feel that I should get out, but I can't. I have no money to speak of, and I rely on Cade to take care of me financially. However, we are planning an art exhibition of my water-colours shortly. If I sell any, I would like to put the money away and try to build an emergency fund."

"Maybe I can also help you there," said Liza. "Cade doesn't know it, but I have some gold coins locked away in a bank safe. I would be happy for you to take them and sell them."

"I... I couldn't. They belong to you and you may need them."

"I'm an old lady, who already has all her needs met. I will never get the opportunity to sell that gold or use the money. You forget, I'm trapped here. Perhaps this will make up in some small way for all you have suffered at the hands of my son. If I can help you escape, then I will feel as if I have done something to put right the terrible wrongs he has done."

"How would we do this?"

"I'll give you a signed letter, plus the password and combination number, along with a certified copy of my identity book; present those to the bank to gain access to the account. Then take the coins and sell them. Easy as that. I promise, there will be no problems."

"Well… if you're sure, it would be extremely beneficial. But I still feel uncomfortable about it."

"You don't need to decide today. Next time you see me, I will have the letter ready. You can make your decision then. Think of it as the inheritance that would have gone to my grandchildren."

"Thank you, Liza; I will give it careful consideration. I promise to visit you again. Now, I feel sad leaving you here, especially knowing that there is nothing wrong with you. That Cade blackmailed you into living in this facility."

"Don't you worry about me, dear, I am content. I am so pleased to have met you, Amber, and I'd like to assist you in any way I can. I wish I could help Cade, but considering matters realistically, I think it's too late for me to do anything. You may still be able to, although, I'm not sure how."

"I don't know either. I would like to find out if Cade is still being treated for his condition and if anything else can be done. I know this must sound strange, but I love him and hate him at the same time. When he's kind and caring, I love him dearly. On the other hand, when he's angry and abusive I hate him desperately."

"I know how you feel; I felt the same with his father. I believe he was also Bipolar. Of course, he was never diagnosed or treated, as it was a different time. The result was that he made our lives a living hell. It was also much worse when he drank, and to be frank, I was glad when he died because life became so much easier without him."

Eventually, it was time for me to leave, I needed to be home before Cade got there. I promised Liza that I would revisit her as soon as I could. As I drove away, a million thoughts went through my head. Even though I had received answers to many questions, the day also left me with more queries than I would ever have imagined.

My first thought was to tackle Cade yet again about the paintings in the storeroom, and also to see if we could bring this Bipolar disorder out into the open. However, I decided that it was prudent to wait until I had some money in the bank and plans in place, just in case things turned ugly.

Chapter 25

A month after I got to know Cade's mother, we held my first art exhibition at the same place where I had met Cade, on the Hout Bay Beach. After that day, my paintings would be on display in the gallery. I hoped that some of my work sold at the first showing, so that I could get money in the bank.

I worked frantically for four weeks and completed some of the best water-colours I had ever painted. I did not see much of Cade during this time of preparation, and he did not seem to be bothered by it. I guess he understood what was happening, as he had done this many times before with his own art displays. It was a relief anyway, because that way I did not have to explain my change in attitude towards him, or broach the subject of his disorder before I was ready.

It was a lovely spring morning on the day of the showing and we had an excellent turnout. Some of my Varsity friends came to the exhibition and were very complimentary. But although a good few hours had passed and people seemed to be impressed, no one had bought anything.

There was a lull in the crowd, and I took a wander past all the easels, examining the layout. It was not working, all the paintings faced the sun, and it was washing out the colours. I decided to turn them until they were backlit and that made the work look infinitely better.

That turned out to be a perfect decision because with the next wave of art lovers, I sold half a dozen pieces in two hours and felt incredibly elated. By the end of the afternoon, I had only a few pieces left, and a sizeable nest egg in my pocket.

Cade seemed to be just as enthusiastic as I was about my success.

My concern now was, what was I going to send to the gallery?

Cade was unfazed and suggested I add some of my recent oil and gouache experimental works to the collection, and as I painted more pieces, he would hang them in the gallery. Indeed, he saw there was going to be a demand for my work and encouraged me to get painting.

I got so busy over the next while that he and I hardly saw each other. I also realised that six months had passed since I last saw Liza and felt guilty I had not been back since.

One weekend, while Cade was away travelling and promoting our art at various galleries across the country, I decided to go and see Elizabeth Raine again.

She was delighted to see me and understood why I had not yet returned.

During our conversation, I told her that I was building a nice little nest egg and, that while I was touched by her kind and most generous offer, I didn't think it would be necessary for me to cash in her gold coins.

Liza was happy that things were going well, both with the sales of my paintings and our marriage, albeit because we saw so little of each other. I took some photographic prints of some of mine and Cade's artwork, and she was touched by the thought and impressed with the talent she saw. She was also pleased that Cade's popular work displayed none of the macabre elements she had seen previously.

We had a lovely afternoon together and again I was sad that she could not be more involved in our lives. As excellent as it was, I definitely did not comprehend why Cade had put her in this facility. She could just as effortlessly have lived in a retirement home, or even with us. Liza was easy to get on with and obviously still loved her son. She just did not understand him, and he had no time for her.

There was not much I could do about the situation and mentioned the fact that I had not seen any of my own family in years, and had hardly any friends, on Cade's insistence.

Liza told me that her husband had done the same; isolated her from family, friends, and any kind of social life. She found out later, as did I, that this is a standard method used by abusers to control their subjects. Hence, Cade had grown up in an abusive and utterly dysfunctional home.

I felt pity for my husband, and as so many women are inclined to do, wanted to fix this "broken bird" in my life. Exactly how I was going to accomplish that, I did not know. I thought I should see if I could find any medication he might be taking and broach the subject from that point of view.

Liza agreed that sounded like a good plan of action and it would leave her out of the scenario.

It was not as simple as I thought because Cade was very cagey and secretive and I did not want him to catch me snooping through his things. I waited patiently for the chance to investigate, and it finally presented itself when he announced that he was going to visit his mother. For some reason, he left his briefcase at home and surprisingly, unlocked. Evidently, I knew he was not going to see Liza, but chose not to confront him, giving me the perfect opportunity to check for medication. I carefully opened his briefcase, and there it was, a bottle of pills lying right on top.

I checked the prescription date on the container, and it was only a few weeks old, so I felt some relief that he was taking his meds. I also made a note of the doctor's name and planned to look up his information, so that I could keep a phone number and address on hand, just in case.

In any event, I still had the dilemma of confronting him with my knowledge, and I gave the situation a great deal of thought. I tried to figure out how I was going to do that without him discovering that I had rummaged through his belongings.

Then it struck me. I would "accidentally" knock the briefcase off his desk, from where he had left it perched across the corner. I made up a story that I was chasing a bird that flew into the house and bumped it by accident.

I did exactly that, hitting the briefcase with some force. It tumbled to the floor, spilling its contents, including the pill container. I even went so far as to collect a few birds' feathers from the garden to authenticate my fib, dropped them in the study and waited for Cade to come home.

When I heard the car pulling into the driveway, I quickly ran to the study and opened the door into the garden. I did this, first to give credence to my story about the bird, as if I had just shooed it outside, but also to provide me with an escape route if things turned nasty.

In one hand, I held the pill container, and in the other, I had a tea towel. I stood in the open doorway, looking out into the garden and pretended to be out of breath when Cade entered the room. I had strategically placed chairs between us as if I had moved them in my frantic attempt to catch the bird.

"What the hell happened here?" he shouted.

I spoke as quickly as I could, trying to diffuse his rising anger. "A bird flew through the house and into your study," I lied. "I ran to open the door and chase it out, but it kept flying around. I knocked your briefcase off the desk trying to get to it… I have just managed to shoo it into the garden."

Cade had a stunned and confused look on his face. His anger seemed to be subsiding until he noticed the container in my hand. His eyes filled with fury, hands balled into fists at his sides, and his mouth became a thin hard line.

I began to quiver with fear, but stood my ground behind the large study chairs blocking his path to the door. "What are these for? Please tell me if there is something wrong. I am here if you need me."

He stood poised, balanced on the balls of his feet, like a boxer about to move into action. Then the fire in his eyes dimmed slightly, and he cocked his head to one side, as if taking in what I said.

Pleading with him to listen to me, I whispered, "Cade, you are my husband, and I am concerned about you. Let me in, and you won't have to do this alone. Whatever the problem is, I will be beside you. I am your wife. I love you… you can trust me."

Without warning, he collapsed into one of the big wing-back chairs, his face in his hands, and started crying as if his heart would break.

Momentarily stunned, I paused in the doorway. Then, I ran to my husband, knelt at his feet, and held him tightly in my arms.

Between sobs, he began to tell me what he was going through with the disorder. That he was under the care of a psychologist and a psychiatrist, who had prescribed the medication and believed it was effective and helping him cope with everyday life.

I gently broached the subject of his drinking. "Cade, I would think that alcohol and this prescription are not a good mix, so why do you drink?"

"I hate that my life is controlled by a disease and the drugs necessary to deal with it. Sometimes I just want to let go and do what I like."

"I can understand letting go a little. But why don't you stop after a glass or two? When the bottle is finished, so are you. You become a different person, violent, and abusive."

"I know, and I am sorry. It's a compulsion. Once I've had the first glass, any thought of stopping goes out the window. I try to control it, I truly do. Logically, I know the drugs and drink combined get the better of me. When alcohol takes hold of me, I lose all inhibitions. I don't ever intend to hurt you, Amber. Surely you know that?"

"Part of me does. But you have in the past, and because of it, we lost our baby. I can never have more children. You took that away from me!"

Cade stared at me with a sad, haunted look in his eyes and I could see a lifetime of anguish written all over his face. The thought came to me, "hurting people hurt people".

"I honestly didn't mean to," he muttered. "And I will never forgive myself for causing you so much sorrow. How do we move forward from here?"

"I'm not sure. One day at a time I guess."

Cade and I sat together in the study as the shadows lengthened across the wall, holding each other close. We stayed that way for a long, long time, lost in our thoughts until night fell and we were shrouded in darkness.

Chapter 26

Weeks passed by and things were going well between us. In fact, much better since the night we spoke in the study. Even so, I still felt as if a sword dangled precariously over my head and it could drop at any moment. I walked on eggshells around my husband, frequently biting my tongue, so that I would not blurt out anything I did not want him to know.

I longed to talk to him about his mother, and confront him about the paintings in the storeroom, but I was still very afraid and lacked courage. The day would come when I had to deal with these things, because they were eating me inside, but not yet. Instead, I became obsessed with spending hours in the shed outside, staring at the macabre artworks and trying to get inside Cade's head.

I could understand the manic and depressive states of the disease to a certain extent, however, I was not able to get my mind around the dreadfully dark and sadistic nature of his paintings. There were many that turned my stomach, apart from the one depicting hell. A particular piece fascinated me, in spite of its appalling content. A naked cherub-like little boy was being grasped by the foot and dragged down into a dark hole spewing fire. Only the evil creature's hideous hand holding onto the baby's foot was visible, the only perceptible clue as to the demon's identity pulling the child into that hell-like place. It was a bony, repulsive black claw, with curved nails an inch long, which dug deep into the boy's flesh.

Then the day came, Cade surprised me by returning home early and caught me off-guard, studying that specific piece in the outside storeroom.

He became livid in an instant. "Amber, what are you doing in here? I told you to never come into this room. How did you get the key?"

I could not think fast enough to give him a plausible answer.

In his rage, he picked up the canvas, which was block-mounted, and struck me with it. A vicious blow across the face, knocking me to the floor and leaving me dazed.

I reeled from the attack, dizzy and disoriented, my mind coming to a standstill. All I could do was scramble away into the far corner, behind some of the paintings, to get away from my husband.

Cade tossed heavy framed and block-mounted canvasses out of his way like matchsticks, still wielding the picture of hell above his head like a weapon. Just as he brought down its full force towards me, I lifted a painting in the corner and used it as a shield. In a split second, I realised it was my broken portrait. The one he had slashed to pieces. The one he denied ever completing.

As he stepped back to take another swipe at me, I pulled the dustsheet off the piece and thrust it at him.

Momentarily side-tracked, he stopped in mid-stride, and stared open-mouthed at the hacked canvas.

"Why did you do this? What made you slice me? The portrait you said you never finished? I don't understand. Tell me Cade, why?"

He looked confused and bewildered for a moment and without answering me, dropped the shattered painting of the boy being dragged into Hell and staggered out into the garden.

Cautiously, I followed him, standing a distance away, and saw his body was set as hard as stone. I could feel anger coming off him in waves and decided to make a run for it, rather than continue the confrontation.

I disappeared into the house and locked myself in the en-suite bathroom. My heart pounded, and I shook all over. I took a long drink of cold water from the tap to calm myself, then splashed some on my face, and sat down on the floor, with my back against the wall furthest away from the door.

It felt as if hours passed, but locked in the bathroom, I had no way of knowing what time it was. I knew that I had not heard his car leave, so I was sure he was still around and felt too afraid to venture out to check. There was a sudden sharp knock on the door, and I jumped with fright.

"Amber, I am genuinely sorry I lost my temper. I have calmed down now, please come out of the bathroom. We can talk, and I will explain everything."

"I don't know if I can trust you. You keep hurting me, and I am afraid of you. Just leave. When I hear your car drive away, I will come out."

"I don't want to hurt you anymore, my Love. If you listen to me, I will tell you why I painted those dreadful images, and the reason I never wanted you to see them."

I stood silently praying for a few seconds then decided to take the risk and open the door. Whatever had happened or was about to happen, I needed the truth. I felt compelled to discover what had twisted his mind so badly.

Cade was sitting in a chair at the bay window, elbows on his knees, and his head in his hands. He looked up as I walked towards him then indicated that I should sit in the other chair, and hear him out. Wearily he said, "Where do I even begin?"

"Start at the beginning, where you believe things changed and brought you down this awful path."

"I don't remember much before I was three or nearly four-years-old, but it must have started early when my father cruelly abused me. If I didn't do things exactly as he told me to do, he would beat me until I could not walk. Sometimes,

I didn't even know what I had done wrong. As if that wasn't bad enough, he used to pick me up by the throat and throttle me until I lost consciousness. While he did these things, he also told me what a horrid little boy I was and that one day I would end up in hell. He seemed to take pleasure in describing that place to me, filled with evil demons and all-consuming fire. He would gleefully tell me the devil himself was going to come for me. I was terrified. Day and night, that was all I could think about, the devil pulling me into the fire."

I was stupefied and felt sobs choking my throat. I could not imagine any father doing that to his son, especially my husband. Liza had shown me photographs of him as a young boy, and he had looked like a blond cherub. The thought of any parent willingly hurting their own child made me extremely angry. "Is that why you started drawing pictures of the abyss?"

Cade gave me a strange look.

I realised what I had said and that he would wonder how I knew, so I continued quickly, hoping he wouldn't call me on it. "Is that why you painted hell, demons, and the devil?"

"Yes, partly, but there is something else as well. I honestly believe that I may have been dead for a few seconds on one occasion when my Dad strangled me because that was the vision I saw. In later years, I believed I went to hell that day and that was where I belonged, especially after my father died. I thought I was a very bad boy, who deserved to be punished. I used to have dreams about being in that horrific place, and the only thing that gave me any relief was drawing or painting the scenes and getting them out of my head, even if only temporarily."

My heart broke in that moment of confession and once more I reached out to my suffering husband, pulling him into my arms to comfort him, as tears ran silently down our cheeks. The painting of the cherub-like little boy being dragged into hell finally made sense.

Another painting that had horrified me was a gigantic, looming evil figure, with arms raised and a mouth breathing what looked like fire that filled the entire canvas. The creature towered over a small tow-haired boy, who was crouching low on the ground with a petrified look on his face. Now, I understood. Cade was the frightened child and his father, the giant monster. What a tragedy.

I was devastated by the loss of our daughter, but Cade had lived through hell, and struggled daily against his abusive father's legacy. It was indeed a miracle that he had survived. The question remained, where did we go from here?

I had gained some insight into Cade's unbalanced mind, but I was not at all sure I wanted to live the rest of my life with an abusive man, no matter how loving he could be at times. He seemed to be filled with equal amounts of love, hate, and extreme rage. As I pondered on the life of this broken and gravely damaged human being beside me, I began to realise that there was no way I could help or fix him. However, there was still something else I needed to know. "Cade, please tell me why you ruined the portrait you painted of me?"

He didn't answer for a while, then slowly and hesitantly, began. "I… I hated it. When it was completed… you looked so beautiful, so perfect. At that moment, I loathed you, for everything in my life that was ugly, deformed, and imperfect. I did not want to take my frustration out on you, so instead, I slashed your face in the painting. Perhaps I thought that making you look hideous would somehow heal my torment. It never could. It never did. I was still in agony inside and kept taking it out on you! That desecrated portrait was a constant reminder of all my flaws and failures, which is why I hid it at the back of the storeroom, in the corner."

Once more, we sat quietly holding hands. These frightening revelations had taught me so much more about my poor husband, but I did not know how we were going to move ahead from this point.

I did know one thing, I had to talk to Cade's mother again. I had a lot more answers now, but with them had come even more questions, that only she could answer.

Chapter 27

Cade and I spent many hours talking about his illness, childhood, and the death of his father. Discussing the trauma he had experienced at the hand of a parent who should have nurtured and protected him.

He took me out to the storeroom, and we went through the paintings together. I learned about the torture that had birthed each one.

I was glad that my husband was finally opening up to me, but even so, I could sense that he had not told me everything. There were still many secrets that I might never hear about, hidden within his soul.

Months passed before I found an opportunity to visit Elizabeth. I still did not want Cade to know about the time I spent with his mother, as I did not know how he would react to the information. So yet again, I waited until he was out of town before driving up to Constantia.

Liza was delighted to see me and threw her arms around me in a tight hug. "How have you been?"

I was touched and told her, "I'm doing okay, and you?"

"A lot better for seeing you. I have been thinking about you a great deal these past few months. I always fear that something may have happened when I haven't seen you for a while."

"Well, Cade has gone out of town for a few days and I try to come visit you when he's not around. I have no idea what he would do if he discovered that we know each other."

"I worry about that too, although, I don't think it's likely, unless he becomes suspicious for some reason. Cade hasn't been to see me in the last sixteen years, so I doubt he'll be over anytime soon."

"I agree. But now and then he disappears and goes someplace on the occasions he says he's coming to see you. I have no clue where he is, what he's doing, or what he's hiding, and I don't want to take chances either. I thought he might be going to see his psychiatrist. He told me about him, so I don't understand why he continues to lie. He still says he's coming to visit you."

"Tell me what has happened, and did you find out anything about Cade's medication?"

"Quite a few things have transpired since I last saw you."

I then proceeded to share about our skirmish in the storeroom, the study confrontation and his medication, as well as Cade's subsequent revelations about his father and the paintings.

Liza pretty much knew most of what I told her, except for the fact that Cade believed he had died and come back to life when his father strangled him into submission. She sat crying softly with her hands folded in her lap, rubbing them constantly over each other in distress. "I am so sorry that I did not do more for my son. I know that I was not in my right mind due to my husband's manipulation and treatment of me, his emotional abuse. Still, that is no excuse. As a mother, I should have taken better care of my child."

"Liza, maybe you could have done more, but truthfully, the blame lies squarely on the shoulders of Cade's father. He abused him, not you."

"I let it happen!"

"You were being abused too, and you speak now from safety. How much could you really do?"

"Not much I suppose. But I feel so guilty for not doing more." Then she asked curiously, "What happened to the dreadful paintings after he caught you looking at them?"

"We looked at them together, and he explained his rationale behind each one. Then, he burnt them," I replied. "Made a huge bonfire in the back garden and set them all alight."

"So that was the end of them? No more hellish art?"

"I don't honestly know. Cade bought a new padlock for the door and has been much more careful to keep that key hidden. He is definitely concealing something out there. It could be more artwork, but whatever it is, he does not want me to see it." We sat together in silence for a while, then I said, "I do have one important question to ask today."

"Ask anything, I will answer as best I can."

"What happened to your husband? How did he die?"

Liza stared out the window for a long time before responding. "Cade's father was a creature of habit. Every night he spent time in the upstairs sitting room, drank a few whiskies while he smoked a cigar, and read the newspaper. When he was done, he switched off the light, and walked downstairs to the bedroom in the dark. One night, Cade was lying at the top of the landing when his father stepped out of the lounge, tripped over him, and fell down the stairs. He landed on his head, and I believe died instantly. When I came running out of my room, I saw Brick lying in a pool of blood, with Cade standing over him like a little marble statue in the moonlight. I asked him what had happened and he told me."

"I didn't mean to hurt Daddy. Is he going to be okay, Mommy?"

"I held him close and told him never to say anything to anyone about what happened. But I will never know if he lay there on purpose waiting for his dad in the dark, or if it was purely an accident." Elizabeth started to cry noisily.

I comforted her with a hug, pressing a hanky into her hand to stem the tears, and encouraged her to continue.

Between sobs she said, "I called the police and did not mention that Brick tripped over Cade on the way down the stairs. I did, however, tell them that he had been drinking, and concluded that he probably stumbled and fell. They must have believed me because the funeral took place and nothing further was investigated. The coroner had done a blood test, which found high levels of alcohol in his bloodstream, so they left it at that. Cade and I never spoke of it again."

The story gave me chills, and I was shivering noticeably by the time Liza finished. I asked. "If Cade did not lie at the top of the staircase on purpose, why else would he be there?"

"I wondered about it many times over the years. Then comforted myself with the thought that perhaps Cade simply wanted to be close to his father. He was not allowed in the sitting room after supper, so the nearest he could get was the landing outside the door." Liza shrugged despondently.

"That would make sense if Cade had a typical relationship with his dad and wanted to spend time with him. But his father abused and tortured him, so that would not be the case. It's more likely that he kept his distance and perhaps even hid himself so Brick could not see or find him." I pointed out.

"You're probably right, I'm just a silly old woman who wanted to believe the best of her son. I was abused by Brick as well, who expertly manipulated me. I lost all confidence and self-esteem, and honestly, I did not function effectively on any level for years. I was simply in survival mode and going on basic instinct. I wanted to protect my son, but the best I could manage to do was pretend that nothing was happening. I failed him miserably."

"Don't be too hard on yourself, Liza, it's easy to be critical in retrospect. Perhaps you could have done something to protect your son, but it is also possible that things may have turned worse, and you are the one who might have been killed, instead of the other way around. In a sense, it can be argued that Cade was protecting both of you by causing Brick's death, if that is what actually happened. So, unless your son confesses, one way or the other, we will never know the truth. Personally, I baulk from confronting him on this one!"

"I agree, because if he didn't do it intentionally, then he might feel guilty by association, just for being in the wrong place at the wrong time. However, if he did it on purpose, your own life could be at stake. Amber, I still think you should get out. I fear terribly that Cade will snap one day and you could end up dead."

"I am very conflicted, Liza. I feel bad for Cade because of his illness, and for the little boy trapped within, who was so badly abused… I want to help him."

"Candidly, I don't think you can. He needs further professional support, not just pills, and I don't see Cade agreeing to it. Remember, he's also a self-absorbed narcissist, who does not take any criticism well. Plus, he is a master manipulator, just like daddy. He would twist things around, and have the doctor thinking you are the crazy one, not him."

"I promise I'll consider all you have told me. Strange you should say so because sometimes, I do think I'm the one who is nuts and not thinking straight. I do feel sorry for my husband and part of me loves him a great deal, nonetheless, I know he is dangerous. Cade has hurt me badly in the past, both in body and soul and even though I have forgiven him, I have never forgotten. I know that kind of abuse is not justified under any circumstances and I should not make excuses, yet, there is something inside me that wants to fix this "broken bird". Maybe I should get some psychological help myself."

"Whatever you decide, I'll be there for you. I will stand behind you and support you in the decision you make.

And my offer of gold coins still stands, I will help you in any way I can."

"Thank you, Liza. I have come to care for you dearly, and I will come see you again as soon as possible."

"I love you too, Amber. Take good care of yourself."

On the drive home, I pondered honestly over my relationship with Cade. The whole situation was tricky and complicated and I did not know how to approach it. I finally understood more about my husband, his past, especially where it involved his father and his daily torment, and my heart was once more softened. I wanted to find some way to help him, although, it seemed like an utterly impossible task.

Chapter 28

With a renewed mind-set, and determined to try help Cade get well, I worked hard on our marriage. I did my best to forgive all that had gone before and to move forward positively.

My husband also seemed to be making a supreme effort to keep himself on an even keel. He was taking his medication correctly and abstained from consuming excess alcohol. Weeks passed without him getting angry or abusive.

I began to feel secure enough and happy with my life. The weeks became months, in fact, a couple of years passed trouble free, and everything was going quite well. I loved my husband, even more now because of what I knew he had been through. There had been no drama or outbursts for some time, and I began to relax and believe, despite everything I had learned from my mother-in-law, and our history, that we could have a good future together.

He booked us into Champagne Castle in the Drakensberg for a long weekend, to celebrate our ten-year wedding anniversary, as we had originally planned to do some years before.

I wanted to buy Cade something special to mark the occasion, and I explored online for ideas. The traditional gift for the tenth anniversary used to be something made from tin or aluminium, however, the modern trend has become diamonds. I wanted to find an item incorporating both those elements.

I combed the internet in search of the perfect gift and found a beautiful Italian watch. The strap was black alligator leather, the watch-case made of aluminium, and the face included diamonds; a large one marked the twelve and three smaller ones placed on the three, six, and nine. It came in a beautiful black-leather zip-up case. I decided to have a silver plaque attached to the back of the case engraved with the words "My Forever Love", and the date of our wedding.

The watch was very lavish, but I was not concerned, as I finally had savings in the bank from the sale of my paintings. In all the years of marriage, Cade had been the one spoiling me with beautiful gifts, so I wanted to do something unusual for him, now that I had money of my own. I was incredibly excited and could barely wait to go away for our weekend in the mountains and give him his gift.

As we got closer to our mini-vacation, I began to wonder how Cade planned for us to get to our destination. He had not mentioned plane tickets, and it was a long way to drive from the Cape. However, on the Friday morning, when we were due to depart for our trip, he pulled the BMW SUV out of the garage, and I thought that was how we were travelling.

To my surprise, not long after we left home, he pulled into the shoreline parking area in Hout Bay. I looked at him quizzically, curious as to why we had stopped there, but he just sat and smiled at me, an enigmatic look on his face.

I did not have long to ponder, because after a couple of minutes, I heard a helicopter, which landed right in front of us, on the beach.

"Let's go," said Cade, and taking one suitcase in each hand, he sprinted across the sand.

I followed as quickly as I could.

Out of the helicopter, leapt one of Cade's assistants from the art gallery, and Cade handed him the car and house keys after he helped load our luggage. I realised he was returning to our home with the car, and would apparently be house-sitting for the weekend.

With an enormous grin on his face, Cade looked at me and said, "Surprise!"

I smiled back happily. "This is wonderful. The view from up here is gorgeous!"

We took off over the bay and flew along the Chapman's Peak route for a couple of minutes before the pilot swung around and began to travel inland to our destination. Cade and I sat holding hands like high-school sweethearts, watching the swiftly moving scenes before our eyes.

It felt like a short flight before the scenery below became rugged and mountainous, with a wild beauty all its own. The pilot put the helicopter down on the helipad right on the hotel grounds.

Cade removed our luggage and shook hands with the man, after confirming arrangements to collect us on Monday morning. Then once more grabbing both suitcases, he moved quickly towards the hotel.

I trotted along behind him, trying to drink in the beauty around me. The trees were turning green with spring leaves, the grass was thick and luxurious, the immaculate gardens surrounded a crystal-clear swimming pool, and the mountains were behind us.

We made our way to the reception area, and Cade booked us into our suite, which was a Deluxe mountain-facing room with a private patio and luxury amenities.

After quickly unpacking our suitcases and taking a walk through the grounds towards the dining room, which served a buffet-style breakfast, lunch, and dinner, we went to have something to eat. The view of the Drakensberg Mountains through the big picture-windows was magnificent.

It was too late in the day to go hiking, as it still gets dark early in springtime on the berg. So instead, Cade and I explored our surroundings. We took a walk down the long driveway to the road entrance and saw the beautiful Azalea bushes in bloom. They were as lovely as I had imagined, in shades of red, cerise, magenta, yellow, white, and peach. We even took a walk along the road to stretch our legs.

Then we headed back towards the dining area where we sat on the veranda overlooking the swimming pool. We enjoyed a delightful afternoon coffee, with freshly baked scones, strawberry jam, and whipped cream. Afterwards, we decided to take a nap.

Later on, towards evening, we enjoyed sundowners with other guests, before once more returning to the dining room for a delectable buffet dinner.

After supper, Cade and I retired to the formal lounge, where a toasty fire burned, as the evening was slightly chilly. We sat opposite each other, in front of the fire, relaxing in large wing-back chairs and sipping sherry.

The next day was the actual date of our wedding anniversary, but I knew Cade wanted to go hiking early and I didn't want to rush my gift-giving in the morning. I had stowed the parcel away in my handbag. This was the ideal opportunity to present the watch to my husband, and I did so with a joyful grin.

Cade seemed pleased that I bought him something special to mark the occasion and a look of delight came over his face as he drew the engraved watch out of its leather pouch. "This is very handsome, Amber, thank you for the thoughtful gift. I will treasure it forever and always be reminded of this day, whenever I check the time."

I blushed like a teenage girl and smiled happily. "I am glad you like it," I said and explained the meaning of the aluminium for the old, and diamonds for the new wedding anniversary traditions.

We walked back to our luxury suite hand-in-hand, absorbing the ambience of the dark night with millions of brilliant stars shining in the black velvet sky. Thankfully,

Cade had limited himself to two alcoholic drinks and not over-indulged. That night, he made love to me so tenderly, I almost forgot he could also be a vicious monster, and fell in love with my husband all over again.

Early next morning, we arose refreshed, and donned our hiking gear. Cade had picked up a map from reception when we arrived, and we were planning to hike to Crystal Falls. In a small backpack, we placed bottles of water, protein bars, a first aid kit, and our cell phones. Then we went to enjoy a hearty breakfast in the restaurant before heading into the mountains.

The walk took us a good couple of hours. At a certain point, we reached the height where we could look back on the hotel and out over the valley. The views were amazing. We took plenty of photographs as keepsakes.

When we arrived at the Crystal Falls, they were flowing well, due to the increased rainfall the area had experienced in past weeks. The waterfall cascaded from the mountain above into an ice-cold pond below. It was lovely to freshen up in the water after a hot and dusty hike.

Cade and I sat on a rock under a tree, enjoying the sounds of the falling water and nature around us. We munched on protein bars and sipped on water we had collected from the ice-cold mountain spray.

He pulled a small wrapped package out of the backpack and presented it to me with a theatrical flourish. "Your wedding anniversary gift, my lady!"

Smiling appreciatively, I quickly opened the present, charmed that my husband had also bought me something. I stuffed the paper and ribbon back in the bag and opened the red velvet box. Nestled inside was the most beautiful eternity ring I had ever seen. I gasped with astonishment and placed one hand over my heart. "Oh, Cade! It is exquisite!"

Cade took the circle of brilliant diamonds set in gold out of its holder and seizing my left hand said, "May I?"

I just nodded, too choked up to speak, tears filling my eyes. After he placed the gorgeous ring on my finger, I flung my arms around his neck and kissed him passionately. "Thank you, my Love," I exclaimed breathlessly. "This is one of the loveliest gift I have ever received, and I will never forget this moment or this wonderful weekend."

Cade pulled me up onto my feet, kissed me back, and suggested we head back to the hotel for lunch.

Afterwards, Cade arranged for a car with the hotel staff, and we drove to the Thokoziza Restaurant and Delicatessen. In the shopping centre, we enjoyed browsing through the arts and crafts shops, buying some small souvenirs, and then enjoying some special coffee and cake at Thokoziza. We returned to the hotel just in time to freshen up and change for dinner.

To our surprise, there was a complimentary bottle of French Champagne chilling at our table in a silver ice bucket. The accompanying card congratulated us on our ten-year wedding anniversary and offered best wishes. After supper, a dance was organised by the hotel staff, and Cade and I spent the rest of the evening in each other's arms, enjoying the romance of a perfect night.

Much later, when we retired to bed, I took off my gorgeous new eternity ring and examined the diamonds, which sparkled in the light like the stars in the night sky. As I placed it in the trinket box with the rest of my jewellery, I noticed an engraving on the inside of the gold band. It was the initials C and A entwined and our wedding date alongside. Once more, I felt tender tears well up. 'Cade does love me,' I thought, and my heart did a little happy dance inside.

Next morning dawned all too quickly, as it was already our last day away. We both slept in late, exhausted from our busy-ness the day before. We scrambled to get dressed and make it to the dining room for breakfast before it closed.

I was a bit stiff and sore from our previous day's hike, so after some discussion, we decided to take a shorter route called, "Mike's Path." This walk more-or-less followed the river, and while there were a few ups-and-downs, it was easy enough and ended in a field with a small lake. After enjoying the view for a while, we returned to the hotel in time for lunch. That afternoon, we decided to relax by the swimming pool. I enjoyed soaking up the warm rays, while Cade braved the chilly water for a bracing swim.

Then we changed back into our comfortable clothes to enjoy afternoon tea, which was crumpets served with maple syrup and whipped cream. We sat outside on the veranda absorbing the fabulous view, breathing in the fresh mountain air, and sipping our coffee.

The hotel manager wandered over to chat and ended up spending some time sitting with us at our table. He wanted to know if we had enjoyed our stay and we assured him that we had loved every minute of it. Cade also remembered to thank him warmly for the bottle of champagne. Time flew by so quickly, and before we knew it, we had to excuse ourselves to get ready for supper.

Sunday was our last night, as we were flying out after breakfast the next morning, so we packed our suitcases and made sure we were organised to leave the following day.

Cade and I retired early and planned to get up to view the sunrise, however, when we looked out of the window there was a morning mist so dense, we could not even see the mountain. I was a bit concerned about how the helicopter would land, but after a couple of hours the thick white blanket lifted and the day was bright and clear.

We had a late breakfast, and there was just time for one last walk around the beautiful grounds before our pilot arrived to collect us.

As we took off into the air and flew low over the Drakensberg, we looked down on a striking sight of green and ruggedness, with a few high mountain peaks still covered in snow. And we both knew this was a weekend we would never forget.

Chapter 29

At this point, it would have been the perfect ending to a love story, if I could claim that we lived happily ever after. But this is not that tale, and once more, things took a turn for the worse.

We returned to the routine of daily life after our glorious weekend away, and everything seemed fine until the morning I went to pay for the watch I had bought Cade online with my credit card. I went into the bank to draw the money out of my account only to be told by the bank clerk that it was completely empty, there was not a single cent left.

I was astounded! I had tens of thousands in my little stash, or so I believed. What could have happened to my money? Shocked and livid, I asked to speak to the Bank Manager, whom I had only met on one prior occasion.

Mrs Steele came out and greeted me warmly, inviting me into her office. "Please sit down," she said, "and tell me your problem."

I explained in a flurry of confused words about the money I had been saving, that it was all gone, and I had no idea how that could be, because I, Amber Raine, had not touched it.

The Manager looked surprised and confused. "Mrs Raine, your husband was in here a few weeks ago and withdrew all the money out of that account."

Now it was my turn to look confused. "How is that p-possible?" I stuttered.

Mrs Steele answered, "Mr Raine came into the bank with an affidavit signed by you, giving him permission to draw a bank guaranteed cheque, which he said you were planning to invest. Everything appeared to be in order, and your signature matched our database, so we complied with his request."

I was too stunned to respond or even cry, my mind a chaotic flood of thoughts. Then I managed to say, "Thank you for your help." I grabbed my bag and ran out, shaking uncontrollably all the way to the car. I sat there in the driver's seat, with my face in my hands, weeping.

I should have known it was too good to be true to last. I had foolishly clung to my romantic dreams. Initially, I could not comprehend. 'Why has Cade done this?' Everything was going along splendidly, so why would my husband steal my money? An answer came to mind immediately, and I knew for sure in my gut that it was the correct one. He evidently felt threatened by my growing financial independence and had taken matters into his own hands. Nothing else made sense, as he had been extremely generous to me over the years. Why would he take all my money? He obviously needed to control me through my finances.

Absolutely devoid of ideas what to do next, I found myself driving in the direction of Constantia and decided to go see Cade's Mother, and confide to her what had happened.

Liza was pleased to see me, as she usually was. Nevertheless, she also knew instantly that something was amiss.

I described to her our wedding anniversary weekend, showed her the incredible diamond eternity ring Cade had given me, and told her about the watch I had presented to him. Then I revealed his blatant betrayal of trust, that he had stolen all my money from my bank account.

Liza did not even bat an eyelid, hardly shocked about the revelation, and shook her head, as if trying to wake up from a nightmare. "Amber, I want you to take these documents to my bank and collect the gold coins," she said as she took an envelope from a drawer. "But be careful, and sell only one at a time, so as not to invite any unwanted attention from the authorities by selling a bunch at once. That money will help you pay off your debt and start afresh with a new bank account, at a new bank. Don't tell Cade about it, and pretend that everything is fine."

I did not want to take Liza's gold coin collection, but on the other hand, as things stood, I had no choice. Unless I wanted to be thousands in debt, and that would only sink me farther into the morass, my husband was ostensibly planning for me. I had to pay that credit card, then get rid of it. At last, I conceded, it was time to make a concrete plan to get out.

All these years I had fooled myself into thinking that Cade and I had a proper marriage, that we could genuinely be soulmates, and life partners. Instead, he was everything I abhorred; an abuser, as well as a fraudster, and a thief. I knew deep in my heart that I had only loved a shell; the person inside Cade was not the man I thought I married and he had lied and manipulated me from the beginning. I was just stupid enough to fall for it and even to think I could have helped him was utterly ludicrous.

With paperwork in hand, I went straight to my mother-in-law's bank to pick up her gold coins. Everything was in order, and the clerk did not even look surprised at my request. I realised at that moment, how easy it was for Cade to steal my money. The only thing that confused me was how he had managed to forge my signature so perfectly that no one had even become suspicious of any wrongdoing.

I cast my mind back, trying to remember when last I had signed anything in Cade's presence. At first, I drew a blank. Then I began to recall a day, not long after we started planning my first exhibition. Cade had brought over some paperwork for insurance purposes on my paintings, which he said I had to sign and he would submit on my behalf. I had not doubted him or thought much about it, but at this moment, it seemed like the most likely opportunity he had to get my signature. I had scribbled many pages and not even checked them, much less read them, so whether he forged my name or used one of those papers, signed by me, the result had been the same.

It was true, I was an idiot, and far too trusting. But all that was about to change.

I went to a jeweller directly and sold one of the coins. That enabled me to settle the credit card, and I resolved to spend the next few months, slowly selling off the rest to the various jewellers spread around the province, until I had acquired enough money to replace my nest egg and I could leave. I was done with this sham of a marriage.

A few weeks later I sold another coin and opened an account in Constantia at a different bank. Afterwards, I popped in to see Liza again, explained what I had been doing, and what my plans were for the future.

She was sad things had turned out this way, more for my sake than Cade's, as she seemed to have given up on him a long time ago.

If there was anyone on this God-given earth who could understand what I had already been through, my current position, and what I had to do now, it was her, and I was grateful for that.

Chapter 30

It was time for changes, but more importantly, to move on with my life. It had taken ten years, but in a single moment, I had complete clarity about the reality of my situation. Cade was sick, and I was wretched about that, but I finally admitted to myself, I could not help him. My husband was not merely ill with something that could be controlled by pills and willpower, he was, for all intents and purposes, certifiably insane, and that was unquestionably something I could not fix. Indeed, that was a job for One much greater than I.

I secretly began putting my plans together to exit the marriage and get as far away as I could from Cade. I knew that—as surely as I lived and breathed—he would come after me and possibly kill me for leaving. He had never actually said that to me, but his actions spoke louder than words.

It occurred to me then that I would probably have to emigrate to escape. Fortunately, I had a British Passport, thanks to my parents, and imagined it might be easy enough to move to the United Kingdom if it came to that. Thus, my first step was to gather as much money as I could from Liza's coins and keep it safe, together with my new British and current South African passports.

I intended to hide the balance of the coins in a safe place with my passports, however, they were nowhere to be found. I searched diligently throughout the house, but could not locate them. The last time they had been used was when

Cade and I went on our cruise, and now that I thought about it, I had not seen them since.

I decided not mention that I was looking for them, and merely reapply for new ones. Even if Cade had them in his possession for safe-keeping or some other reasonable excuse, I could unintentionally tip him off to my escape plot. On the other hand, if he was hiding them on purpose, then that was much more sinister and dangerous, and I deemed it wise not to confront him.

Whenever possible, I took drives to towns near and far, in order to sell the coins at various collectors' shops and jewellers. I parted with them one at a time, as instructed by Liza, so as not to draw unnecessary attention. They were worth a great deal of money, and although it was time-consuming, I was building up another decent stash, my escape fund.

Any time Cade went out of town, I headed in the opposite direction, and went to see Liza as often as I could. I kept her up-to-date on all my plans, and she was immensely pleased that I was doing something positive with her help. I knew she was devastated about Cade's outcome and his slippery slope future, but I was also fully aware that she considered helping me to be a kind of redemption for her failure to protect him as a young boy.

I understood how she felt, because I too had wanted to save Cade from himself, and somehow, miraculously make him all better. What I discovered was that it was not possible for me to fix another human being. Instead, I needed to save myself.

It was in the telling of my life story to Liza that I could see a condensed version of my existence, as if under a microscope, and unexpectedly, it was illuminated with light and clarity. It dawned on me that I had been fighting a losing battle for years, pushing against the tide, and unable to make any progress.

I bought a GPS, so I did not need to programme the one in my car, on the off-chance Cade checked it to see where I had been. I kept it hidden when not in use, and I also purchased various maps of South Africa and Great Britain. I was, frankly, preparing for a life on the run, and even though it was going to be extremely hard, my instincts told me this drastic step was necessary.

There were days when I thought Cade must surely know what I was planning, as if he somehow could read my mind, and he did seem to sense that I was behaving oddly, no matter how much I tried to act normally. But I was also terrified that I would inadvertently set him off and he might kill me in a fit of rage, long before I could even drive out of the yard, so I tried to be discreet. Slowly but surely, everything started coming together, and I began to believe that I could make a clean getaway. I was sure he would never suspect I was leaving him and I would be long gone before he could ever find me.

I bought myself an iPad and new iPhone, so I could connect to the internet anywhere, anytime. If I were on the run, I could book plane tickets and do other online transactions, without needing to be on our home computer. I hid those, along with the money, and my two new passports when they arrived.

I considered turning to my sister, Crystal, for assistance, but I worried Cade would correctly assume that I had gone there and hurt her or her family, so I decided it was best to leave her out of everything. Fortunately, he knew nothing about Crystal, either her surname or address, except that she lived in White River. Maybe I could get together with my brother, Lane, if he still lived in England, and he might be able to help me, although, I was not very optimistic about that either.

I packed what I called the "go bag" with my necessary documents, cash, and balance of the gold coins. I put in some light jeans, underwear, extra socks, and a thin sweater, plus another all-weather jacket. There was also a small toiletry holder, filled with essentials. I was ready to go at a moment's notice. I hid the backpack at the bottom of the laundry hamper because I felt quite confident that was the last place Cade would ever look for anything.

With a plan in place, all I needed to decide was when to leave. Then, Cade announced he was going out of town for a few days, and I determined that that would be the day. Unfortunately, it was also the day when all hell broke loose.

On the first day he was gone, I went to Liza's home one last time, to say goodbye.

She was sad to see me go and we shed tears together and hugged for a long time.

I then returned home to pack one bag I could manage on my own and prepared to leave the next morning. Feeling pleased with the arrangements, I enjoyed my last evening in the house. Taking a bubble bath and drinking sherry, while listening to classical music.

I went to bed and was reading a new book before retiring for the night, when I heard Cade's car in the driveway. Why was he home? Something was wrong. At that very moment, my cell phone rang.

It was Liza. "Amber, get out, get out now!" She cried hysterically into the phone. "Cade knows, he must have followed you here today and came to see me. He hurt me, Amber, and he's going to kill you. Please, Honey, leave now, and don't look back."

I whispered, "He's here, Liza. I must go. Love you."

I switched off the phone, shoved it into my handbag, and quickly hid my suitcase in the cupboard. Then I carried on reading my book, pretending I had been completely absorbed, and had not heard anything, when he walked in.

All my pretence was to no avail because unmistakeably, Cade did know. He stormed into the room, picked me up like a ragdoll, and flung me around in an alcohol-fuelled rage. How he did not kill me outright, I will never know, because at one point he strangled me until I passed out. He punched and kicked me severely, fracturing a couple of ribs. I am convinced he left me for dead…

"And there you have it, Gloria, my long, depressing story."

"Oh, my dear, my heart breaks for you." She said with tears in her eyes. "It is a devastating tale indeed. I am so sorry to hear about all you have endured, as well as the loss of your precious daughter. You have great strength of character and you cannot regret the fact that you wanted to do the loving thing."

"Thank you for saying that, Gloria. I have so many regrets. Even so, I do know that I did everything in my power to help Cade and make my marriage work."

"Yes, you did. Now, you have managed to get away, and that is all that matters. Why don't you go and freshen up before you leave?"

Amber stood up and gave Gloria a grateful hug. "I'll do that. Just be a few minutes." Then she walked down the passage, into the bathroom, wiped her eyes, and blew her nose. She splashed some cold water on her face, patted it dry, and smoothed down her hair.

Afterwards, she went to collect her backpack, before returning to the kitchen.

Chapter 31

Amber placed a generous amount of money on the bedside pedestal then she glanced around the room one more time. Feeling satisfied she had packed everything that belonged to her, she opened the bedroom curtains and looked out at the view. Parked in the street outside, she could just make out a red Ferrari in the early morning light. It felt as if her heart lurched violently up into her throat and she began to shake uncontrollably.

'That can't be Cade.' Her mind whirled. Surely, he could not have found her so soon.

Just then, her tall, handsome husband climbed out of the car and looked around, as if trying to decide which direction to take.

Amber did not hesitate a second longer. Running as fast as she could, she dashed into the kitchen and grabbed Gloria's hand. "My husband is here… he's found me! Cade is standing next to his car, right outside in the street. Please, help me. Is there another way out of the parking area?"

"Yes, there is." Gloria answered, also alarmed. "Go out the door you came in last night. Drive your car through the hanging creepers, to the other side of the Pergola, and turn immediately left onto the dirt road. You can drive through the vineyards until you reach the next intersecting road and turn left again. That will take you onto a back road, and you can travel straight inland, turn right to East London, or left back towards Cape Town. Go quickly. And if your

177

husband knocks on my door, I will stall him for as long as possible. Go now, and God be with you."

Amber picked up her things, ran out the door in a panic, and dropped the car keys as she went. Her broken ribs screamed with pain as she bent down to desperately grab them. On the other side of the house, the roar of a powerful engine kicked in. Cade was on his way, and she had to move fast. Frantically, she searched for the key and jumped into the bronze SUV as quickly as she could. Thankfully, despite the cold and rain, the engine started immediately, and she followed Gloria's instructions, driving out through the Pergola and onto the dusty road.

Just as Amber pushed the vehicle through the hanging vines, she heard the Ferrari to her right and knew Cade had found the driveway to Gloria's cottage. Praying for God to protect her, and Gloria, she drove hastily through the vineyards.

'How on earth did he find me so quickly? Is it feasible he tracked the vehicle's GPS… or even my cell phone?'

She needed to put as many miles as possible between them, ditch the car, and destroy the phone. Just as she thought it, Amber grabbed the small gadget, took it apart, and threw the pieces out the window. Then, she reached for the new iPhone she had secretly bought and activated some months earlier. She switched it on and tapped into Google for directions.

At the main intersection, Amber chose to turn left and head back towards Port Elizabeth, for now was the time to put an alternative plan into action. She followed the GPS to the highway, and ninety minutes later she arrived at her destination.

She dumped the SUV close to the main road, out of sight behind a building, and grabbing her luggage, headed to Affordable Car Hire just outside of town, her "go bag" on her back, and pulling the suitcase along on its wheels.

As it turned out, there was a pretty young blonde, with Britt engraved on her nametag, working behind the counter. As Amber walked in, she took off her sunglasses and turned her face, looking straight into Britt's eyes for full impact.

Britt gasped at the sight of the black eye and swollen split lip, which were now completely devoid of make-up and incredibly obvious.

Amber played on her sympathy, begging the young woman to deny that she had ever seen her if Cade came looking. Then she went further, telling Britt how her husband was abusing her, had threatened to kill her; that she was trying to get away… As it was all true, it was also totally believable, and Britt swore to keep Amber's secret.

Climbing gingerly into the silver VW Jetta, Amber plugged in her iPhone and headed for Beaufort West. She prayed Cade would assume she had continued travelling north, towards East London, and that could buy her some precious time.

Four and a half hours later, Amber arrived in Beaufort West. She drove to the railway station and quickly parked the car. She had arranged with Britt, for a fee, for someone to collect the Jetta and return it to Port Elizabeth. Then she went to the ticket office for Rovos Rail, bought a ticket to Cape Town at a hefty price, as she was not travelling from the origination point, and left the Jetta keys in an envelope with the office staff to be collected by the Affordable Car Hire representative.

The train was leaving in minutes, and Amber scrambled to make it in time, running awkwardly along the platform with her luggage, to get on-board before it departed without her. She arrived breathing heavily from nerves and pure physical exertion, clutching her damaged ribcage with both arms to minimise the pain.

On the luxury train, Amber was allocated a Deluxe suite, where she could freshen up, and afterwards enjoy a meal in the beautifully-appointed dining car. The ride was going to take eight hours, she had some time to think and plan her next move. She was also able to sit in the comfort and quiet of a private suite and gaze out at the beautiful scenery passing by.

Gloria had given Amber her phone number, and she decided that now was a good time to give her a call and hear what had transpired with Cade's unexpected arrival.

She answered on the first ring. "Hello? Gloria McBride speaking."

"Hi, Gloria, it's Amber."

"Oh, Amber, Honey, how are you doing?"

"I'm okay for the moment. Please tell me what happened with Cade this morning."

"Well, seconds after you left, his Ferrari pulled into my driveway. I kept praying that you had got away safely. I made him wait outside for a while before I answered the door. Even so, he was very charming and pleasant, so I thought I should invite him in, to delay him further."

"Oh, Gloria, are you okay? Did he hurt you?"

"No, I'm fine. He came in, and I offered him coffee, which he accepted and sat in the kitchen with me while I made it. I guess he imagined you were in the house and that he had plenty of time to find you. Anyhow, I managed to keep him chatting for about an hour. I admitted that you had been here but left before he arrived. I told him you were going to East London. I hope you went in a different direction."

"I did. In fact, I doubled back and returned to Cape Town. I am on my way there by train right now. Do you think he bought your story that I was heading towards East London?"

"I think so because he drove away in that direction. I did buy you at least sixty minutes, maybe more, I hope it was enough."

"Me too, Gloria. Thank you for everything you have done for me. I left money to cover my room and board for last night on the bedside pedestal in the room where I slept."

"That wasn't necessary, Amber, I am so glad I could help you."

"I know, and I'm very grateful for your kindness. Buy yourself something special and think of me."

"Indeed, I will."

"When I'm somewhere safe, I will call you again. God bless."

"You too, Honey. Take care of yourself. I will be praying for you. Goodbye."

After she called Gloria, Amber decided to call Liza, to see how she was doing.

The phone rang a while, before Elizabeth answered hesitantly, "Hello…"

"Liza, it's me, Amber. I have a new cell phone number now."

"Oh, thank goodness, Amber. I have been so worried about you. Are you okay?"

"He beat me quite severely this time, Liza. I have a few broken ribs, black eye, split lip, and multiple bruises. Cade even strangled me at one point, until I passed out. When my body was limp and lifeless in his hands, he threw me across the room and left. Even after all he has done, I could not believe he almost killed me."

"I am so sorry, precious girl," Liza whispered tearfully.

"Are you alright, Elizabeth?"

"Better now. A couple of bruises on my upper arms, where Cade grabbed me. He shook me very hard and hurt my neck. I became frightened when he threatened to kill me… I'm sorry, but he forced me to confess everything. About your planned escape; that you were going to get out of the country… Please tell me what happened after I saw you on Thursday."

"Well… I left your place, went home, and got everything packed and ready to depart Friday morning. Unfortunately, Cade somehow figured out something was up, and came to see you."

"He followed you here, told me so."

"Then he was unquestionably suspicious."

"Oh, yes."

"I wonder what tipped him off? And I have to wonder now if he followed me on previous occasions when I visited you. Perhaps telling me he was going away for weekends was a ruse to cover the fact that he was trying to find out what I was doing?"

"Cade is very clever and cunning, and somehow, always seems to be one step ahead."

"Indeed, it's really petrifying. After he left me for dead, I may have been unconscious for hours. When I came around, I managed to get myself to the bathroom to get cleaned up. I was badly injured, so I took painkillers and tried to get some rest, hoping and praying, he would not come back. I slept curled up on the floor, then pull myself together, and left Friday morning. I took the coast road, before heading onto the highway and up to Port Elizabeth. It took me longer than I would have liked, but since Cade was going to be in Cape Town, it made sense to keep away from there. My first stop was at Heidelberg to fill up with petrol. Went through Port Elizabeth, filled up the tank again, then to Grahamstown, and drove for a couple of hours on the other side. By then it was dark, and I needed a place to spend the night, or I was going to make a bed in the SUV. But I happened across this timeworn sign advertising bed and breakfast. It belonged to a dear old lady, called Gloria McBride. I was very grateful that she took me in."

"That was fortunate. It would not have been safe to sleep in your car."

"I suppose. Gloria was very good to me, gave me food and drink and a comfortable place to sleep. She also listened to my miserable life story. I think hearing me relate what I suffered at Cade's hand encouraged her to help me."

"What did she do?"

"Believe it or not, Cade found me at that way-out little place."

"Oh, no! What happened?"

"This morning, I looked out the window and saw his car in the street. That's when I realised he was following me. I told Gloria and she gave me an alternative route to get out of the parking area and onto a back road through the vineyards. While I was making my escape, she invited Cade inside and kept him talking for an hour. That gave me a good head start. So I headed back to Cape Town. Hiring a rental car and then hopping aboard this train. I hope Cade continues driving to East London, and that will give me time to get to the airport and catch the first flight out to England."

"I hope your plan works, Amber. I shall be thinking of you."

"Thank you, Liza. I pray you stay safe. That Cade won't come back to hurt you again."

"I alerted the security staff after he left and they won't let him in here again. I am sure I will be protected. Anyhow, I'm no use to him now that you're gone. I doubt he will ever pay any more attention to me."

"Hopefully, that's true. I'd better go now, Elizabeth. I will make a plan to contact you once I'm safely in the UK. I dearly love you, and I am sad to say goodbye."

"All I want is for you to have a good life, Honey. Don't worry about me. Look after yourself. Bye, Amber."

"Goodbye, Liza."

After completing the call with Elizabeth Raine, Amber sat ruminating over the day's events. Cade had found her far too quickly, and effortlessly, and that did not bode well for the future. Would she ever escape his clutches? She felt anger rise. He had her on the run, because there was no way she was ever returning to a life with him.

The next step in her carefully thought-out strategy was the one she wished she would never have to make. Once she had finished the train section of her journey, she would catch a taxi to Cape Town airport and see if she could get on the first flight to London. She loathed him even more now that he was forcing her to leave her beloved country.

Chapter 32

As evening drew near, Amber watched the most beautiful sunset from her luxurious train suite. The evening sky was ablaze with glorious shades of orange and red, enhanced by the remnants of rain clouds. It reminded her of many of the prior and significant sunsets she had experienced over the ten years of her marriage to Cade. She gave an involuntary shiver.

Feeling entirely exhausted, she ordered dinner to be brought to the suite and ate a delicious meal in peace, as she soaked up the beautiful South African scenery. She decided to forego the complimentary glass of bubbly that accompanied her dinner, feeling that instead, she needed to have all her wits about her. And combining pills with alcohol would not be wise.

After supper, she took a hot shower, before dressing in fresh clothes, ready to travel by air to England. The warm water was soothing on her aching body, and she hoped that her broken ribs would not cause her too much discomfort on the long flight. Fortunately, she could now afford first class, thanks to Liza Raine's gold coins, so that should help her cope with the tedious journey.

The train trip gave her some rest and respite, and she felt somewhat rejuvenated by the time the train pulled into the Cape Town station. Quickly hailing a taxi, she was on her way through the city and off to the airport in no time at all.

The vehicle was heading out of town to the highway when the traffic came to a grinding halt. Since it was late in the evening and after peak hour traffic, Amber could not understand why they were not moving. She asked the driver if he had any idea what was happening ahead? He replied that he had just listened to a traffic report; there was an accident on the highway, possibly due to the rain.

Amber's heart sank. If she did not get to the airport soon, she would not get on a flight out of the city tonight. So far, it was likely she was way ahead of Cade and without her cell phone and car, he would not be able to track her. But if for any reason, he turned back to Cape Town, he might suspect her intentions and catch her at the airport.

While she waited impatiently for the traffic to move, she decided to purchase an air ticket online, using her iPad, in the hope of expediting time at the airport, and improve her chances of getting on a flight as planned.

Amber unpacked items out of her "go bag" so she could get her passports, in case she needed them for the online booking. They were not there. After taking out every single item and checking repeatedly, she realised that her passports, as well as her new nest egg, and the balance of the gold coins, were no longer in the backpack. Waves of panic and anger rose within her in equal measures. It dawned on her then that there was no way she was going to fly anywhere tonight, not without the necessary documentation.

'Where are all my things?'

The only conclusion she came to was that Cade had somehow, for whatever purpose, dug in the laundry basket, found her bag, and removed the items. Which also meant that he had been onto her plan sooner than she thought. That might also explain why he followed her to see Liza. Cade had cottoned on to the fact that she had set aside money, and her passports, with emergency items for a quick getaway. Since he did not know the timing, he must have decided to follow her around to figure out what she was doing. Of course, once he followed her to his mother and hurt Liza to get information, he knew everything, even the route she planned to take, and the fact that she was going to fly to Britain.

'How could I be so stupid? I should have never told Liza anything. And I can't believe he hurt his own mother.'

Amber sat thinking for a while, her mind chaotic, disjointed, searching for a solution, and making a supreme effort not to panic. Otherwise, there would be no logic in anything she attempted to do, as she tried to beat him at his own game. Swiftly, she came to a decision. She would head back to the house and check if, by some stroke of luck, Cade had left her passports and money at home, and not taken them with him while he chased after her.

If he had travelled on to East London, it did not seem likely that he would drive over eleven hours straight back to Hout Bay. Particularly, if he had lost her trail and been unable to track her cell phone after its destruction. Even if he managed to find her abandoned car in Port Elizabeth, he would have to do some serious detective work to discover where she had gone. It would take him some time to unravel the plot and discover Amber had backtracked. She figured he would also be exhausted, travelling through the night to find her, and surely, he would not be able to do it all over again non-stop, might spend the night somewhere, and start his search again the following day. That would give her time to get away.

Comforting herself with those positive thoughts, Amber instructed the taxi driver to turn around at the first opportunity and take her to the address she gave him in Hout Bay. The man seemed happy to get moving and deliver his client to her destination, so he too could head back home himself.

When Amber arrived back at the place she used to call home, she paid the taxi driver, who took her luggage out of the boot, and deposited it unceremoniously on the driveway.

She opened the garage door with the remote she still had in her handbag, dragged her suitcase out of the rain, and unlocked the door between the garage and kitchen with the key she had absentmindedly pocketed during her departure.

It was hard to believe that only thirty-six hours had passed since Cade had so violently assaulted her because it felt like an eternity.

Amber spent the next few hours turning the house upside down trying to find her documents, gold coins, and money. Then the thought finally came to her to look in the locked drawer of his desk in the study. Grabbing a tool from the garage, and now more desperate than afraid, she broke the lock open. There they were, all the missing items from her "go bag", as well as her old passports.

Sitting down on the nearest chair, faint, and weak from tension and physical exertion, Amber felt relief flood her body, as she realised that she could still follow her plan, even if it was too late to go now, and she still had to book a flight. On top of it all, she was now utterly exhausted, both physically and emotionally. She proceeded upstairs to the guest bedroom to get some rest—she could not face sleeping in the main bedroom, the place where she had so recently and brutally been attacked. Then she called a taxi to pick her up early in the morning, to head back to the airport.

She prepared for the night, took a couple of painkillers before climbing into the comfortable bed, and fell asleep the instant her head hit the pillow.

Chapter 33

Amber awoke with a start, disoriented in the darkness, and her heart hammering in her chest. Something had disturbed her slumber, and she could not directly identify the cause. She heard the door to the kitchen slam shut, and the grind of the garage motor as the door rolled down. Someone was inside.

She could hear the person moving about, switching on lights, opening kitchen cabinets, and the fridge. She recognised the pattern of those sounds. She had listened to them so many times before, as she lay in bed waiting for him to return from work. It was Cade.

Lying as quiet and still as she could, Amber prayed that she had not left any evidence lying around that would give away the fact that she was in the house. Her mind was foggy from sleep and the effects of painkillers, but the adrenaline coursing through her veins was helping clarify her thoughts super-fast to plan her next move.

Seemingly, Cade had not bought into her deception and come to the realisation that she had headed back to Cape Town, planning to fly out from that airport. Naturally, he would not have found her there, so the logical conclusion was to return home. Hopefully, he did not imagine she was there too, and that might give her an advantage. If he went to bed without venturing upstairs, she could sneak out in the morning when he left to continue the fruitless hunt for his wife.

Luck was not on her side. Amber recollected that she had opened a bottle of water, poured some into a glass, and left the rest in the fridge. Cade was an observant man; he would notice it if he knew what items were in there before he left.

He evidently remembered, and noticed, because she heard him yell, "Shit!" and the sound of the half-empty water bottle being hurled across the room, hitting the far wall. The noise of shattering glass echoed terrifyingly throughout the house.

In an instant, Amber slipped out of bed and hastily pulled up the covers. She decided to move quickly across the upstairs landing and into the sitting room alongside her art studio. She felt sure that if Cade did not find her downstairs and came looking for her, the first place he would go into was the guest room to see if she was sleeping there.

As she crouched down in the corner behind the large comfortable couch in the upstairs lounge, she heard Cade tearing through the house, moving furniture, and tossing things around. There was the sound of more fragile items breaking and then his voice, low and menacing, which struck absolute terror into her heart.

"Amber, I know you are here. Come out, Honey. I just want to talk."

She did not respond. Instead, she looked around in the dark for something with which to arm herself. There was nothing close by, and she dared not twitch a muscle, for fear he would hear the movement and find her in no time. At that moment, her hand touched a velour throw that was draped across the back of the couch. Slowly and silently, she pulled it off, draped it over her body, and curled up as small as she could in the corner. Perhaps, if luck turned her way, her infuriated husband would not notice it.

It took Cade agonisingly long minutes to examine the downstairs rooms, checking cupboards, and even under beds and the bathrooms. All the while, he called her name, beseeching her in a soft, silky tone. "I promise I won't hurt you. I'm sorry for everything, and it will never happen again. Please come out!"

Amber closed her eyes and took a deep breath, trying to still her trembling limbs, and kept praying he would give up looking for her. That he would think he was either mistaken, or that she had already left again.

Inevitably, she heard his footsteps, as he made his way up the marble staircase and onto the landing, switching on lights as he went. He turned right straight away, and she heard him go into the bedroom. When he saw the rumpled bedding, he would know she was still here and hiding somewhere.

Her body froze with fear yet small beads of sweat formed on her brow and upper lip. Trying to focus, she came up with an escape plan; if only Cade did not notice her bundled under the blanket behind the couch.

At last, he entered the sitting room and flicked on the overhead light. By some miracle, it did not go on. The bulb must have blown, and it was the first thing going Amber's way. He marched straight across the lounge in the dark, into her art studio, and to the light switch in there.

That was when Amber made her move and leapt up from behind the couch. She ran for the door, planning to go down the stairs as fast as she could, and get outside in the dark, where it would be harder for him to find her.

Just as she got to the door, Cade flew out of the studio, and tackled her to the floor.

Her broken ribs slammed against the hard surface and caused agonising pain to shoot through her entire body, knocking the wind straight out of her. With adrenaline coursing through her veins, and a strong survival instinct for preservation, it gave her almost super-human strength, and she managed to break free of his grip and pull herself around behind a large lounge chair.

Cade stood upright before advancing on her position, filling the room with his menacing presence, backlit by the studio's light. Then slamming the sitting room door shut, he walked towards her.

With all her might, she shoved the big chair towards him, and it momentarily stopped him in his tracks. She ran behind the other lounge chair and into her art studio, banging the door behind her and looked around frantically for something to keep the door closed.

Before she could even move an item of furniture in front of it, Cade burst into the room, and Amber barely had time to position herself on the far side of her art desk. If he went one way, she went the other.

After a few minutes, Cade, tired of the cat-and-mouse game, tried a different tack. "Amber, why are you running away from me? I promise I won't hurt you ever again. Please, believe me." He sat down in one of the easy chairs in front of the picture window, patting the other opposite him. "Come sit here, and we can talk. I love you, Honey."

Without hesitation, Amber turned and ran to the studio door and yanked it open, moving as fast as her injuries would allow. But she was not quick enough.

In an instant, Cade was right behind her and chasing her through the sitting room.

This time, as he tackled her, and she fell through the doorway and onto the landing. The instinct to self-protect kicked-in, and as he stood up to approach her once more, she rolled over to her right, facing away from the stairs.

In that second two things happened simultaneously. First, there was an almighty clap of thunder, accompanied by a blinding bolt of lightning, and all the lights in the house went out. In an instant, everything went completely black. Then, Cade, racing towards her, caught his foot against her legs, lost his balance, tripped over her prostrate body, and tumbled head-first, down the marble staircase.

Rolling over to her left, Amber saw the dark shadow fall, land on its head at the bottom of the stairs, heard a crack as it struck the hard marble floor, and collapse in a crumpled heap. Within seconds, a pool of blood began to form alongside Cade's temple and spread out around his head, but she could not see that in the dark.

Amber waited for him to move and tentatively called out his name, "Cade? Cade, are you okay?"

There was only silence.

In a state of shock, Amber grabbed the banister, carefully pulled herself upright, and very slowly descended the stairs while clinging to the railing. Her eyes adjusted gradually to the darkness as she went, and she kept them squarely on the still figure lying below. After what seemed like an eternity, she reached the immobile body. Fearing he would suddenly open his eyes and turn around to grab her, she skirted past his feet and moved towards the entrance hall.

She stood there a moment, uncertain what to do next. Should she call emergency services or the police first? But since he had not moved, it was probably advisable she check for a pulse, and then decide. Cautiously, she approached the motionless body and knelt beside him, waiting for a second to see if he stirred, before placing two fingers against the side of his neck. There was no pulse. There was nothing. No sign of life.

Amber felt in Cade's pocket for his cell phone and dialled a number. It rang twice.

"Hello. Who's there?"

"Liza, it's me, Amber."

"Oh, precious girl, are you okay?"

"I'm fine, but I have something to tell you about Cade…"

"What's happened?"

"I think he's dead. He… tumbled down the stairs and landed on his head."

"Oh, my goodness, Amber!" said Liza anxiously. "Are you sure?"

"Yes, he's gone. Please call the police for me. I'm too shaken up to do it myself."

"Of course. I'll get back in touch with you once I have contacted the necessary authorities. Sit tight and try to remain calm. And Amber, it's not your fault, you have nothing to worry about. It was just a dreadful accident."

'Or was it?'

"Thanks, Liza."

"Bye, Dear. I'll talk to you again shortly."

Amber placed the phone back in Cade's pocket then gingerly sat down cross-legged on the floor, carefully lifted his bleeding head into her lap, and gazed down at the inert appearance of her handsome husband.

His left arm had fallen across his body, and she could see the face of his anniversary watch was badly cracked. Lifting his hand up to her eyes, she just made out the time. It read exactly three o'clock in the morning. It had stopped working on impact.

She stared at an object on the floor, something she did not recognise right away. As her eyes adjusted to the darkness, she realised what it was. Cade must have been carrying the watch case in his pocket because it now lay beside him. Amber picked it up to examine it. At that moment, a shaft of moonlight broke between the clouds and shone through the clear-glass window alongside the front door. It illuminated Cade in an ethereal, silvery light.

Slowly, she read the words she had engraved on the outside of the case just months before, "My Forever Love". Then she placed his limp arm back onto his chest and continued to clutch the blood-stained watch case.

Sombrely, she contemplated the lifeless body of her husband. He looked like a carved marble statue of a Greek god, pale, and motionless. A shell of a human being. And then she cried, cried yet again for all she had lost through this man; their daughter, future children, her peace of mind, dignity, self-confidence and even her money. There was nothing that he had not violently taken from her. She shook him wildly with barely concealed rage.

But the moment passed, and filled with regret and remorse, Amber hugged Cade close to her chest, salty tears streaming down her cheeks, unchecked, and dripped silently onto his stone-cold face.

THE END

Barbara Harrison is a woman who loves telling stories. She was an avid reader as a teenager, whose interest in the world of imagination was first stirred by the written word. Barbara started with writing scripts for plays and poetry. This love for words, then extended into a passion for acting and bringing the written word to life. As a hopeless romantic, she mostly enjoyed reading books about "true love" and finding a "soulmate".

As she grew into womanhood, the young Barbara began to realise that sadly, the love stories depicted in "Mills and Boon" novels, were far removed from real life.

In 1988 she married her late husband, Russel Harrison, and they raised two children together. After many marital ups and downs and twelve years of marriage, Russel moved to Florida, USA. This was a huge shock to Barbara and their children, who had no desire to relocate overseas.

For a period of fourteen years. Barbara lived a life of split family on two continents, travelling between America and South Africa.

Tragically, in August 2012, after a mole biopsy on his arm, Russel received news that it had become a melanoma. He recovered well from the surgery to remove the cancer, however, it had spread, and in April 2014 was considered to be stage four and therefore terminal.

Both returned to South Africa in July 2014, where Russ received treatment and they could be with family and friends during that dreadful time. On 1 October 2015, their twenty-seventh wedding anniversary, Russel passed away, leaving Barbara a grieving widow.

Barbara began to slowly move forward again, and as she looked back to take stock of her life, she began to realise that she had spent most of her married life, living her husband's dream. Although she thoroughly enjoyed being a wife and mother, there had been no ambition, other than the love of acting many years ago, to follow a career.

At the age of fifty, encouraged by two of her friends, Barbara began to write again. Her first couple of endeavours were in the non-fiction world and she did not attempt to publish. One of her friends suggested that she try her hand at writing novels. Another friend greatly believed in her ability to write and constantly encouraged her to keep going, ultimately birthing the book you now hold in your hands.

Visit the author's website at
https://barbaraharrisonwrites.wordpress.com/

www.ingramcontent.com/pod-product-compliance
Lightning Source LLC
Chambersburg PA
CBHW070948190726
48292CB00004B/1376

9 781945 286421